RYAN BLOO

FABULOUS RIDERS

FABULOUS RIDERS

RYAN BLOODWORTH

Copyright ©2017 Ryan Bloodworth
All rights reserved.

This book is dedicated to the freedom
of Tibet and Maitreya's vision.

First published in the United Kingdom in 2017
by Ryan Bloodworth.

Fabulous Riders ©2017 Ryan Bloodworth

The right of Ryan Bloodworth to be identified as
author of this work has been asserted by him in
accordance with the Copyright, Design and Patent
Act 1988.

Written by Ryan Bloodworth

British Library Cataloguing-in-Publication Data
A catalogue record for this book is available
from the British Library

All rights reserved. No part of this publication may
be reproduced or transmitted in any form or by any
means, electronic or mechanical, including photocopy,
recording or any other information storage and retrieval
system, without prior permission in writing from the
publisher.

All logos and trademarks used herein are the property
of their respective owners. The use of any trademark in
this book does not vest in the author or publisher any
trademark ownership rights in such trademarks, nor
does the use of such trademarks imply affiliation with
or endorsement of this book by such owners.

ISBN 978-1537735894

Chapter 1

Alex is sitting back deep in his chair with a sullen and disturbed look to him. The room is dimly lit and the curtains are closed; the noise of rush hour traffic emits an impersonal noise against the windows. He sits in silence and stares blankly towards the floor. The silence is not still but has a haunted and unsettled feel to it. Alex is an impressive looking man with well-defined cheek bones and a muscular build. He is unwashed and unkempt. He holds a cigarette to his mouth and slowly closes his lips around it before exhaling a rush of smoke. His look is that of shock – that he has encountered some kind of reckoning in his life.

"You ok man?" He asks me with a slow slur.

"Yeah man I'm alright."

"Thanks for coming round man. I appreciate it."

"No problem mate." I look at Alex with concern. There is silence.

He is distant and seems to drift into other thoughts.

"I'm not well." He tells me. The room goes silent again. Alex smokes a cigarette. "I need help man. A nightmare has taken hold of my life." He purses his lips and draws on the cigarette.

I have known Alex for many years since the clubbing days of the 90s; to my mind he was the coolest man on the planet – a leading DJ who always had the best tunes that no one else could get hold of. He was cooler than cool and people felt good around him. We come from different backgrounds. I come from the wealthy home-counties and public school whereas Alex comes from the rough streets of South London; but we met through the music and a strong bond was formed.

The pioneers of dance music were black guys from the US and here in London. They had discovered a new future in the latest technology that they manipulated to create hitherto unintentional sound. They applied their creative minds to the technology and forced out wild and dangerous vibes that blew peoples' minds. Somehow the technology of the West had connected with the African psyche – a whole new world poured out of the speakers that spoke of an ancient past whilst also dreaming of an imagined future. To my mind – these guys hadn't just discovered a sound – they had forced open the cosmic doors to the future.

I think it is still quite unusual for people with such different backgrounds to be friends even though it is increasingly less so these days. If it weren't for the music in the 90s there's no way we would have encountered one another. The music broke down doors and barriers between people. In the ecstasy fuelled nights of 90s clubbing culture the bloke that might have bottled you down the pub was now hugging you like a long lost friend. It was the same with the black guys. The music called people together from all walks of life and for the first time we all danced together vibing off the new sound.

Even in the midst of summer love I was still slightly afraid and in awe of these black guys who seemed from another planet. They were tall, muscular, and seemed to embody the funk of the music. There is no doubt that these guys were pioneers who derived incredible futuristic sounds from the rudimental technology.

With music coming over from the US they held the party together with cutting edge beats that sent the crowd onto another level. I got to know Alex when I started to make some tunes and I would talk to people in the know how to get my records played. Eventually I got to meet Alex who liked the hard-core tunes I was making. As the summer months moved on into years we all developed a friendship meeting up at the cutting houses and record shops. The scene was rocking and there seemed to be no end in sight. We are E.

Alex sits there staring aimlessly in front of him. There is nothing to look at but the dust covered carpet. He sits in old worn out clothes and intermittently flicks the ash of his cigarette in the ashtray. The TV is constantly on and the lights of the screen flash back and forth across the room. The sound is on mute and we sit there together in silence. I don't think Alex is aware of the long silences and sometimes I think he forgets that I am there.

"It's the haters," he tells me. "They have come for payment. They've come for their dues. You know what I mean?"

"The haters. Yeah I know what you mean."

I sit back in my chair and think deeply about what he is telling me. Silence fills the room again. Coloured lights dart across the room from the TV. Alex leans forward staring at the floor with both hands covering his face. I lean to turn a lamp on as dusk slowly falls and it casts a shadow across him revealing the definition of his high cheek bones. He is a physically impressive man – but he casts a forlorn figure as he seems to drift between two worlds. There are moments when he looks up at me animated and laughs a disturbed thought and then he seeps back into a shadow world where the landscape is dark and frightening.

Psychiatry is a dangerous science and I know now that Alex will be drawn into this world by the men in white coats. I fear for him. He sits withdrawn deep in the sofa and looks blankly to the floor. The psychiatrist is another enemy to confront. There is no easy way to do this. Alex is going in to battle. They will call him mad and insane; they will demonise every aspect of his behaviour – even the way he breathes. But this is a battle he must face and the warrior soul stares unblinking at the floor preparing for war.

The psychiatrist is ready to pounce on any show of authentic human emotion. It is our gut that tells us something is wrong with the world. It is our deep-seated feelings and intuition that drive us to break free from the false world. This is the experience of the African diaspora in the West since the years of slavery. For over four hundred years the black man has been vilified for showing authentic human emotion – for reacting instinctively against the false demonization of their behaviour. The African slave was treated as sub-human by the West.

The ignorant Western mind deemed the African an inferior being and treated the rebellious behaviour of slaves as some kind of bestial instinct. The African was reacting to the wicked imprisonment of his soul by these white devils. The African soul despite the horrendous conditions it faced remained rebellious and refused to give in to the false idols of the Western mind.

The West believed in reason – that reason is the only idol to be worshipped. The African lacked reason and their rebellious behaviour only confirmed that these were a primitive people. The white devil stands aboard his ship and throws the African bodies in the hull like beasts and sails with his pompous nose poking upwards. The West is succumb to the cult of reason and believes itself to be superior to all of nature. Deep in the hull the African psyche lies still and rests in a pool of bloody filth awaiting its destination.

The doorbell rings and my heart starts to pound anxiously. Alex barely moves. He sits with heavy limbs drawing slowly on his cigarette. There is a black atmosphere around us and Alex is convulsed by a dark heavy cloud. He is withdrawn and tired but he draws on his cigarette with a determined mind ready for the enemy to strike.

I get up to answer the door revealing a rather plump young woman with a beaming chirpy smile who assertively tells me her name and that she is here to see Alex. I let her in. She steps in with her little chubby feet and has a quick sniff and gaze around the living room. Alex sits motionless huddled in the shadows. He does not look up or make any effort to greet her. The chirpy woman takes it upon herself to sit next to him and introduce herself.

"Hello Alex, I'm the Community Psychiatric Nurse. Your GP has asked me to see how you are. How are you feeling?"

Alex sits darkly in a hidden shadow. The depth of his mind rests deep in his being. He sits silently. He gives no answer.

"Oh dear," the chirpy thing responds, "it seems that you're not feeling very well. I am here to see if I can help you in any way. Now, your GP has requested that we arrange for you to see Dr Brown who is the consultant psychiatrist at the hospital. How does that sound to you Alex?"

With a noble gesture Alex looks up at her and responds that yes ok he will see the psychiatrist. His movements are slow and purposeful. He draws back his gaze and flicks the ash of his cigarette in the ashtray.

"Right." The nurse replies chirpily. "We will send you a letter over the next few days with a date for an appointment." Smoke draws up from the ashtray as Alex stubs his cigarette out and he offers a courteous nod to the woman as she gets up. She leaves as briskly as she came and chirpily says goodbye.

Alex's mood deepens. He looks up at me and gives a dark laugh.

"Good fucking grief."

He withdraws into himself. I am impressed by his immovable courage. He sits still and moves slowly to light up another cigarette.

"Where do we go from here?" He asks me dryly. "So it begins with a little fat woman and an insincere smile. Ha ha ha. Fuckin' hell."

He shifts languidly back into the sofa and rubs his head softly. The gold rings on his fingers glint against the dimly lit room and his gold bracelet moves down his arm as he pinches the skin between his eyes. The hard precious metal belies a hard precious soul and the beauty of the gold speaks of a beauty within. The noble heart of a man is being judged by a chirpy little fat woman.

I see Alex the next day and am pleased that he seems to be feeling a bit better. He is joking with me and pushes and prods me in a playful manner.

"Who are you man? White boy!"

I smile quietly and playfully push him away.

"Yeah white boy's come around here to hear some tunes!" Alex pulls a crisp vinyl record from its sleeve and places it on one of his Technics record players. "Listen to this."

The speakers emit a slow funk sound that builds in rhythm. It is a James Brown track. With cigarette in hand, Alex falls lightly on to the sofa and closes his eyes.

"Funk heals the mind brother." He tells me.

"Yeah man. It certainly does." I reply.

"So what you doin' round here man? Haven't you got anything better to do? No women to see? Ha ha ha!"

"I'm just seeing how you are man."

"Why? You think I need your help? Don't you know my friend this is the life of the black man. Our lives are full of danger. The white slave-trader will never let us free. Go on man, go back to your posh life and leave me alone."

I sit down on the chair next to the sofa saying nothing and refusing to move.

Alex gives out a sinister laugh. We both sit there in silence listening to the record.

"James Brown knew what it was about man." Alex tells me. "Man he went through so much – he went to prison he was fucked up man. He got up and said – I've gotta be James Brown or I'm gonna be nobody."

The funk drives out the speakers. It breaks the stilted air and enlivens the spirit.

"You white boys will never understand. Go back to your pretty boy life."

I don't respond and sit smoking my cigarette. Alex sighs and rubs his forearm against his nose. The gold metal on his arms move dancingly against the grey light outside and as he pulls his arm away from his face his nose stud briefly pierces the smoke that surrounds him with a golden spark.

"Fuckin' white boy coming round here." He mutters to himself.

At this point my patience breaks and I respond that I am his friend and feel he could do with some help right now. He replies with a sniff and an indignant grunt. He rubs his hand intensely over his bald head and face. He is a mighty warrior and a noble spirit in an alien world.

"They're gonna fucking lock me up aren't they?" He tells me. He continues to rub his face and through the haze of smoke he looks at me kindly. "I know you're here to help Nathan and I appreciate that. But what can you do? They just want to lock this nigga up."

The record fades out and Alex gets up to find another one. For a short while, we both sit quietly and listen to the music. The music reaches my soul as much as Alex's. This is the gift of the African diaspora to the West – the music. The music and the vision of the future. You see, we are actually from the same tribe – the future tribe. Ours is an imagined future and the battle is to get there – to bring the future into this world. We are kindred spirits sown from the same seed and we are here on this planet to break it up and bring the funk.

Alex hasn't been out for several days now. He tells me the streets are full of the haters. He is paranoid that every old granny he walks past wants to call the police and he treads a careful path avoiding both the criminals and the law. They are all haters. Cops and robbers – two sides of the same coin. He sits on the sofa breathing in the smoke and meditating on the gathering storm. I sit down with him and we smoke like ancient Native Americans calling on the gods before we strike our enemy.

The haters are close and there is a sense of a black fog seeping in beneath the door and through the windows. The haters are faceless shadows that ease into every corner of the room. They feed off fear; off paranoia. They are the psychiatrist's workers creating darkness wherever they go and the psychiatrist enters like Dracula to feed off his terrified victims. He injects a cold needle into their arms and whispers that he wants to help them. He licks his lips and reacts violently to any dissent. The vampire has you cornered.

The slave trader has dehumanised the African and every cry of rebellion is treated with violent punishment. If you behave yourself Dracula will be kind but dare to call out his venom and he will subdue you with a bite. The haters collect hauntingly in the living room. Alex and I sit there protected by smoke. We watch from afar. We await their move. But they don't move. They just creep in and rest in the dark corners of the room. The postman delivers and there it is – the arranged date to see Dr Brown.

We sit in silence. We are together shoulder to shoulder. The beats pulsate through the speakers and the dub sound sends waves of rhythm through the room. The music awakens our minds to another level. We are on the level of spiritual warriors. The walls of Babylon creak like the rocking hull of the slave ship. The wind and the breaking waves pulsate to a dreaded rhythm that is the tide responding to the movement of the ghost ship. Here we are in the midst of slavery – but our minds are free. You cannot enslave the mind. The dub pressure moves through the living room and our minds awaken to a spiritual energy. We exist on a higher level of consciousness. We sit there unmoved yet together we harness the power that James Brown sang about: soul power.

The room is dimly lit and there is a monotonous hum of traffic outside. It is another grey day and we sit together listening to music. The music speaks to a deeper part of ourselves that goes beyond reason; that enlivens our souls and raises our minds to mystical meditation. The psychiatrist is the high priest of reason crushing any dissent shown by human emotion. The psychiatrist denies the existence of the mind and claims we are the passengers of mere chemistry. The call to Christ and visions of another reality are accused of being delusional and are broken down by way of powerful drugs and physical restraint.

We are chemistry: there is no way out. When a man shows anger or physical rage he is broken down and forced to conform –to reason. Throughout the history of the African diaspora in the West, the high priest of reason has demonised and vilified the behaviour of the black man – to the point that he can't breathe. Police and psychiatric nurses restrain the physical rage of the black man and suffocate him. They kill him. The anaemic pale skin of the psychiatrist has no colour of passion or life – he worships at the altar of rationality and offers the warm blood of a rebellious soul.

The god of reason licks her lips and with ravenous relish she commands the lifeless barbarians in white coats to find more souls to slaughter. The African diaspora are a people full of soul and colour – they express creative music and dance with a deep rhythm to the sound of the universe. They offer a different perspective on reality that contradicts reason – that reality and the universe is far too complex and mysterious to be captured by reason. My friend Alex rides to a deep rhythm – a rhythm deep in nature and space that speaks of an alternative vision.

The slave ships are sent out to capture souls to build western civilisation but little do they realise they are capturing souls that will revolutionise the West and set ablaze the spiritual power of the human soul. The rhythm rides deep – it is unbreakable because it is truth. The universe is a vast ocean of expansive imagination and the renegades of funk dance to the tune of space and imagine a future.

Alex sees me looking at his record collection and he gets up to put something on. He pulls out a well looked after vinyl record that sparkles with static energy and he places it under the needle of the Technics.

The space funk fills the room and our moods lift. The walls of the conventional world break down and we ride high on a space ship in outer space. The rhythm rolls and the beats drive – the synth effects rock and the vibe reaches.

"Ha ha ha. Let's funk this world up!" Alex shouts.

He pulls out a CD and then gently introduces an electronic vibe from Detroit in to the room. We sit back in the creative sound and contemplate our next move. The haters rally at the door and the windows rattle with sinister intent. The ghosts and ghouls fill the air haunting the dark dank pathways. The haters look with cold hateful eyes at the world. All they see is blackness and all they think is poison.

Alex is in a dream land. Surrounded by cigarette smoke and in the low lit room he retreats into a meditation and explores his imagination. He dreams of Africa and the journey his four hundred year old self has been on. He is his people. He is the warrior caught in battle and sold to slave traders. He is the blood-soaked floor of the slave ship and the crying souls that shout terrifyingly into a dark void. The taste of the whip draws a flavour of salt from his blood soaked wound. The women around him shriek and scream afraid of the visions and the hallucinations that they see. The horror of the ghost ship rocks back and forth in the blood red sea.

There is a loud clatter at the window and Alex shudders awake. It is a night of howling winds and violent rainfall. He stares out into his living room. He sees me and offers a warm look. For the psychiatrist there is no reality beyond the apparent material. The visions and powerful rages of the black man are deemed insane and he is chained like a wild beast. But I see in the African mind a kinship and a revelation of the secrets of the universe; that there is a creative force full of infinite potential – that we can imagine a future world and dance to the rhythm of the universe. There is a damp atmosphere to the living room that belies the grey sodden

streets outside. The night is filled with darting blades
and muffled cries.

The doctor is a tall man with dark features. He invites Alex in
with a gallant swing of the arm. He sits before him and with
an insincere smile and the pretence of sanity he asks Alex how
he is feeling. Alex responds that he has been feeling better; but
immediately Dr Brown interrupts him and questions him on his
hallucinations and fits of rage. Alex responds that he has just been
angry and that his visions are artistic and even spiritual in nature.
The doctor courteously acknowledges what he says and makes
some notes. He tells Alex that he wants to bring him in to the
hospital for a few days so that he can reach a better understanding
of the situation. Alex knows that he has no choice. Behind the
meaningless courtesy of Dr Brown is the force and threat of law.
The psychiatrist stands up with a poorly veiled threat of violence
and says that he looks forward to seeing Alex over the next
few days.

We stay up late smoking and listening to music. We listen to the
sound of Coltrane breaking the airwaves with masterful incision.
The cool fracturing of the air reaches into both our minds. It's as if
Coltrane were in the room with us right here and now speaking to
us. His is a sound that originates from the ancient mind of Africa
and soars through the air with a vast wingspan towards the future.
The sound heals our minds and prepares us for the task we face.
Alex sits down deep in the sofa and leans forward covering his
face with his hands. The gold chain around his neck hangs loosely

revealing a cross. He gives a loud sniff and sits up straight rubbing his neck and shoulder. The soft sound of Coltrane quietly ends and Alex gets up to look for another record.

The night draws in and we both sit there in the low light continuing to smoke and listen to the music. The weather outside is vicious and it seems the whole world is absorbed in the terrifying howl of ghosts. Ghosts are that which haunt the mind and enter where darkness lies. Behind the insincere front of the psychiatrist lies a chasm of darkness and ignorance. The dark chasm of the psychiatrist's mind is hidden from view and we face an enemy that wants to understand reality as being made up of some kind of complex neurological wiring. The psychiatrist lacks empathy and has no feeling to the emotion of others. He confronts emotion by breaking it and oppressing it. Much like the slave trader, these idiotic men presume a superiority over nature – that the world can be dominated and the expression of an imaginative alternative reality is to be shut down with violence.

The African psyche is profoundly complex and remarkable. It offers the West an alternative understanding of reality – that rests with nature and not against it. The night gets heavier as we await the morning. Alex goes deep into his mind and imagines a thousand worlds away from here. He is on a boat sailing up stream deep in the forest. He encounters warriors dressed in claret cloth. There is a subtle sound of drums and the warriors draw back the string of their bows. Their knives hang loosely at their hips and with a powerful cry they wake Alex from his dream.

Alex opens his eyes and stares at me. It seems we are surrounded by dark figures and restless spirits. The haters take the form of black shadows and they circle the room giving out screams of laughter and gluttonous thumps on the floor. We both sit back and hold our heads straight. Alex gets up to put a record on. He chooses Voodoo Chile by Hendrix and with a smile and gentle laughter we listen to the sound.

Reality takes on a different form – the banal conventions of a world dominated by reason give way to a majestic vision of an alternative universe – of magic and wonder. Our minds soar the heights of consciousness and sparkle through a thousand worlds. The haters are baffled by the blinding lights of reality and retreat deeper into the hidden corners. Creativity is the source of life.

Alex sifts through a few more records and pulls out electronic sounds. The Detroit and London DJs are heirs to the funk sound and we release our minds to the vibrant and colourful tones of Techno and Drum n Bass. There is a magic to the music that empowers us and creates a zest for life. We await the banal world view of the psychiatrist in the morning but for now we embolden ourselves with the soul and funk of the creative source. Alex laughs out loud and throws me a cigarette. We rest in the sound and envision a future.

The morning comes and we haven't slept. The chirpy little nurse comes to drive Alex to the hospital. I tell him I'll be down to see him. The mighty warrior stands filling the doorway and walks slowly behind miss chirpy into battle.

Chapter 2

Alex sits motionless watching the TV. He is sat next to other patients who are either staring lifelessly towards the floor or moving restlessly unable to settle. There is noise and a cluttering of people darting back and forth across the ward. Seeing him, my heart sinks and I become quite nervous in myself. Standing at the ward entrance I wait several minutes before a nurse notices me and asks who I am here to see. I indicate towards Alex and tell her that I am here to see him.

With a hurried manner the nurse briskly walks me over and peering right into his face with callous empathy she tells Alex that I am here. She looks up at me with an empty smile and leaves me to approach him. I place my hand gently on his shoulder before sitting down. He sits staring at the TV and gives a tired half smile. He still keeps his head shaved and his nose piercing glistens against the light of the TV.

The white of Alex's teeth shine out against his dark features and out of the corner of his mouth without turning to look at me he asks how I am. I reply that I am well and have just come to see how he is doing. As I ask him he gives a sigh full of heavy weariness and he doesn't answer. I don't push him any further and sit in silence watching the TV.

It is almost archetypal now; the serial gameshow host with a false smile projecting into a chaotic hospital ward of broken minds. The TV speaks of a world out there that the patient stares into. The adverts offer a glimpse of a dream world that disappears at the push of a button. Even so, the TV is a tremendous distraction for the patient. It saddens me though that the feigned illusion of a happy life seems to tease the patient that it is a life far away from them.

"I'm heavy man." Alex says to me in a deep and slow London accent. "These drugs just wipe me out."

"Yeah man, I can see that. Are they letting you smoke in here?"

"Yeah, we get allowed out two or three times a day to smoke."

"Well that's something." I reply.

Alex doesn't respond and seems to retreat into his heavy body. He hasn't put on too much weight yet and his muscular physique cuts against the grey atmosphere. The tattoo on his right arm indicates a creative soul that I know refuses to give in. But our conversation does not go much further. He is tired, heavy, and withdrawn. The patients sitting next to us in the TV area seem to be in their own worlds and pay no attention to my presence. The cluttering noise of chairs moving and people busying in the background doesn't seem to affect Alex as he sits deep in himself motionless. I tell him that I'll see him in a couple of days and I lean in to shake his hand; the hard gold of his rings join my hand and his gold bracelet falls back towards his forearm. I press his shoulder with my other hand and look up towards the exit. No one seems to notice me as I make my way out.

The nights are drawing in and the streets are sodden with unrelenting rain. I walk back towards the station and the glowing yellow of the street lamps give a brief glimpse of the dark moving bodies on the pavement. The impersonal groans of the rush hour traffic signify a world veiled in hushed pain; that every mind longs for warmth but finds only the cold stare of a listless society. The pacing bodies tap their oyster cards and we move in sequence towards the platform. The noise of the trains offers a soundtrack to the voiceless journey and I stand tight in the corner listening to the hushed cries of every silent mind.

I switch the sound system on and put on a Detroit album; the complex and intelligent beats calm my mind and seem to reverberate around my living room like Morse code from another brother across the pond. They're out there, I think to myself. There are soulful minds out there creating great art unrecognised by mainstream society.

Despite the lack of recognition, the Detroit producers continue to create incredible music shaping and defining both a futuristic sound and technology. This is what my friendship with Alex is based on – this incredible art form and music that only an African mind could create. I'm not saying white folk can't do funk; I'm saying that this music is the great gift that the African diaspora have given the world. There is nothing like it. Yeah there has been some great rock and folk music throughout the years, but it doesn't compare to this.

From early gospel, jazz, and blues through to hip-hop and House – this black inspired music has shaped and transformed the Western world. Throughout all these music forms there has always been an imagined future and a vision for what the world could be. The parable of Christianity is that Christ died and resurrected offering the world a gift of eternal life: I see the story of the African diaspora in the same light. Suffering, death, and resurrection with the gift of music that invites us to a future promised land.

Gospel sang about it, Coltrane created a sound out of this world, and the pioneers of dance music are the inheritors of this lineage creatively making rich and complex beats using technology to envision a future. The soundscape forms the landscape. Alex is a pioneer who is suffering and through his resurrection he offers the world a magical sound that breaks the old to reveal the new.

Alex's mind is consumed in colour and imagination. He sees the world in a different light and imagines a different landscape. This is a world where there is no death but eternal colour: a dance that rides the contours of the universe. Life and death are just one phase of eternity as the rhythm of space cascades against infinite worlds and infinite possibilities. The stars shine out and the complex pattern of the night sky invites the dreaming soul to think far and deep; that there is a wider ocean to be discovered and endless rhythms to hear. Funk is just that: the rhythm of the universe.

Beyond the ordinary there is a deeper rhythm and a deeper mystery. The brave rider sits tight on his steed and rides the contours and the fine waveforms of the night sky. That the imagination is set free and the power of the creative source bursts through to re-imagine the world. Prodded awake by the podgy spectacled nurse, Alex is told to take his medicine. The unsmiling cold fish pertly moves onto the next patient. And back into the imagination – into outer space. The funk rides on.

With screeching mayhem the chairs of the dining area are pulled back as lunch is prepared. The glum yellow walls peer in towards Alex and the dull reality of hospital lunch pierces his nostrils. Without sound, he languidly moves towards the queue. The bland food is lumped on his plate and he moves down the line to collect his cutlery. Without looking at anyone he sits at an empty table and eats the shit. The radio is on and the cheerful chatter of the disc jockeys distorts into a grating noise of drivel.

The patients consume their food sitting together but alone in their thoughts. The noise of their minds is overbearing but they all sit there with their heads on fire as the useless staff watch the clock. There is no healing here – psychiatry doesn't seek to heal: it seeks to repress. Any behaviour that contradicts the function of utility is deemed an illness. This place is not where a creative mind comes to heal but to survive. The psychiatrist is the enemy of creativity.

The nights are when the nightmares strike. Alex lies on his bed and the door is locked shut. The nurse gives no notice to Alex and without a word leaves him to the dark. The dark is when so much comes alive. The dark invites the ghosts and ghouls and every sound in the corridor outside reverberate a caustic noise of discomfort. It seems everything about the ward tries to imprison the soul; the thick lumpy air chokes the lungs deprived of an open window. The sickly sticky smell of disinfectant and the sterile bareness of the room push and push Alex to crack. But he refuses and he sinks deep into himself.

Alex falls deep into his soul away from the poison of the waking world. He doesn't sleep but he dreams. We are free in our dreams. The imagination is limitless – the outer world dissolves and the soul takes flight in an ocean of symbols. The physical rests on the spiritual and when the door is locked Alex dreams a thousand dreams. He finds solace in the forest – drifting down stream on a narrow wooden boat.

The trees stand tall and their long leaf covered branches reach over the river arching handsomely for the ancient warrior. There is no other movement of life; there is stillness and no sound. The subtle breeze seems to fill him with energy and Alex closes his eyes as the water moves. The rhythm. The rhythm of the water. The boat rises and falls. Everything seems to move as one; in unison like an orchestra. This is the ancient land.

There is a fitful sound of birds calling afar and the hurried rustles of animals foraging the ground. The river meanders left and right always heading in a meaningful direction. Alex keeps his eyes closed and moves with the flow of the water. The breeze is perfectly cool and whispers tales from long distances. The world is one. The night sky opens up and the scattered stars form patterns and weave a language of tales to come. The bright waxing moon rises and emits a cool light that dances majestically on the water's surface.

The dreamer rises from the inner to the outer world. The room is pitch black and several rooms down a man is shouting. He continues to shout when no reply comes. He bangs the door and shouts. Alex lies still with his eyes open listening to the cries. There is muffled movement of footsteps and whispering between nurses. After several minutes the footsteps become firmer and approach the man's room. He shouts and cries. He is troubled and scared. He feels a compulsion to break free – he needs some care.

When all the man receives is a lifeless response from the nurses he is unsatisfied and begins to physically express himself banging on the walls. Alex keeps his mind deep in himself and pities the man for what is about to come. He hears the heavy march of the security guards as they enter the man's room and following a muffled yelp; there is silence as the door is firmly closed and the man lies intoxicated and paralysed. But Alex can still hear his inner cries.

The morning brings no respite and with a curt word the patients are told to get up for breakfast. Alex is slow to rise and rubs his head. He is bleary eyed having not slept and takes a deep breath for the day ahead.

The sharp look and the cutting tone of the psychiatrist's voice hurt Alex as he sits awkwardly on his chair. The nurses surround him with withdrawn gazes and the psychiatrist continues to talk at him like some kind of non-human. Alex is deemed mentally ill and as such his voice is stripped of all power. Everything he says is the expression of the illness and the psychiatrist pushes and probes him into surrender.

"Do you still feel under threat Alex?" The psychiatrist asks.

Alex is reluctant to answer. It is a catch-22. Any expression of his fears and the psychiatrist will pounce with gluttonous glee. The room is void of warmth and Alex feels the sapping feeling of being in an airless vacuum. The psychiatrist pulls tighter and with a hard face he repeats the question.

"No." Alex replies.

The warrior sits among white devils. The lifeless beings stare coldly. In chains the sea becomes a frightening sight. The ghost ship rests sinisterly in the harbour. The blade is pointed sharply in his spine and with noose around his neck he is pushed towards the vessel. Something terrible is happening. A great fear enters his heart. He is powerless. He awaits the fire. Lying tied next to other men, the hull of the ship stinks of death and hellish foreboding. Bodies lie thickly together and there is a collective mourning of minds weighed down by what is to come.

With a flick of the wrist the psychiatrist dismisses Alex and the icy nurses escort him out of the room. In a daze he settles next to a couple of other patients and watches the TV. The cracking noise of raucous voices and scraping chairs fill the room behind him and the intensity of the ward begins to cut him. He drags his hand down his face as the constant chaos of the environment agitates the inner rhythm of his mind. His mind: a deep ocean full of memories and destinies to be fulfilled. There is peace deep down – but he sits exhausted in the intense pressure of the ward.

There is no other way but to walk through the fire. The fire blazes and the walls of the world seem to crumble. All familiarity disappears and the jarring pokes of the nurses prod Alex into movement. They come at him with scowling faces and bent over like witches from fairy tales. They have taken his world and they prod, prod, prod him forcing him to take his medicine.

The ship rises and falls amidst the ocean storm. The hull has an air thick with bodies some of which begin to die and streams of blood get soaked into Alex's clothes. He cannot move but his mind is resolute. The white devils sail the ship through breaking waves and deep down Alex feels the depth of the ocean beneath him. He goes into a dream and seems to break free from the ship. His mind is free –he imagines an empty space which nothing can penetrate yet is the source for everything. The emptiness is full of magical energy and waves of creation.

The rhythm breaks the waves and Alex envisions the fine lines of a subtle reality. He is free and filled with energy: he pulls back the bow and releases an arrow into space. The arrow flies and flies. The rhythm of the death ship breaks against hard water; the loud crashing of the hull drains Alex of his energy. The movement is jagged and inharmonious. It cracks and jerks.

The next few days turn into a blur as Alex takes his medicine – he is subdued but unable to settle his mind. Every touch and every word spoken by the staff jars his stomach. Every action the nurses make is another tightening of the rope. The psychiatrist's voice is like a burning hot needle piercing his flesh. He is enwrapped in a barbaric world where the mind is broken to within an inch of its life.

I feel despair not knowing how to help Alex. I go in to see him and again he is sitting motionless watching the TV. There are other patients next to him each set adrift in their own confused worlds. I rest my hand on his shoulder and ask how he is. He is slow to respond and with a glint of the eyes indicates that somewhere deep within he his riding. He is riding the steed through the confusion of battle where chaos reigns and death wreaks everywhere.

To challenge someone's sanity of mind is the ace card of the enemy. With every movement and every word uttered Alex is tied ever tighter in ropes and chains. He is deemed sub-human and the white devil sails his ship to the Western world; a world where reason is worshipped as the only god. These beasts in the hull lack all reason: their eyes are ablaze with the expression of the subconscious. They see spirits and worship nature as an infinite dream. They stare blankly at the mechanics and coldness of the ship. These devils have come from another world and they capture the soul to be sacrificed at the altar of reason.

Western society moves with the hum of commerce and mechanised efficiency. There is squalor and dirty faces but they all stare at the exotic cargo of the ghost ship. The King sits upon his throne and opines the wealth created by the trade of Africans; these sub-human beasts that have come to the work of the Empire. Alex is ragged with bloodied sweat covering his skin. The grip of the body next to him closes tightly on his arm and there are powerful cries of disturbed minds ricocheting across the hull.

The overseer takes his pick.

Do these beings belong to Christ? The chatter and debate washes through London. The scientifically minded argue no and throw the bodies to their labour. The gentle hearted are ushered away and the message of Christ is forgotten beneath the noise of industrial advancement.

There is no soul; there is only the body. The psychiatrist picks at the mind like a play thing. Here is where fear is located and here is where love is located. You see, this man has a dysfunction of the brain. He imagines things that don't exist and prays to a phantom. He is driven to rage and refuses to conform to our treatment. The further he rebels the tighter we will chain him. The slave falls deep into himself and dreams a different reality. He knows he is being wronged: that is his greatest strength.

Even with the abolition of slavery, the African diaspora continue to suffer the cold bite of scientific reason. The African mind is filled with imagination derived from an ancient past that lived in harmony with the natural world and; filled with rhythm the ancient African envisioned the infinite possibilities of the universe. The spirits of the forest are aspects of the mind that hint at a deeper reality and when sailing the seas the African navigated according to the stars seeing knowledge of other worlds with destinies to be fulfilled.

These psychic powers are crushed by psychiatry; this most barbaric pseudo-science. But it is my belief that it is this wonderful imagination and alternative vision of the world that is the gift of the African mind. Our mind exists as deep as an ocean reaching to what you might call the soul. The psychiatrist is an ignorant beast that lies await on the surface of things and is fooled by how things appear rather than how they are. The psychiatrist does not see the mind. For the psychiatrist there is no mind – just wiring and function. Every action is interpreted within this materialist framework.

Dreams and visions are hallucinations; anger is psychotic; tears are neurosis; insomnia is disturbance. The psychiatrist creeps ever further into Alex's psyche and picks things out looking at them with bemused indifference – the mechanistic mind of the psychiatrist has no understanding of colour, warmth, or feeling. There is no feeling. There is no mind. This man is mentally ill and requires treatment. Alex sits unmoved enwrapped by the web of psychiatry –but the depths of his mind are undisturbed. The depths of his mind glisten against the natural light of the night sky and he rests deeply before rising to the battle.

We put some beats on. Alex sits on the sofa; he is overweight and puffy in his face. His hair has grown a little and he is unkempt. He sinks heavily in to the sofa and wipes his forehead for a few minutes. His gold rings glimmer gently against the daylight.

"You feeling alright man?" I ask.

Alex is slow to answer and with a brief sigh he calmly replies, "yeah man. Yeah man."

I get up to make some tea and bringing the kettle to boil I throw some English Breakfast teabags into the pot. Whilst letting the tea brew, I sit down next to Alex who is staring at the TV. The darting light shapes and contorts Alex's features and hidden behind cigarette smoke I sense that deep down he is ok. The light from the TV flickers and breaks across the room and I get up to pour the tea. For me tea is a wonderful healer; one of the gems of English culture. It has been used for thousands of years not just socially but also in religious ceremonies. Tea is spiritual and it warms the heart. Alex drinks it like any Englishman would; and he places it down carefully on the table with a sigh of gentle relief.

"Cheers man," he says.

We sit together watching the dancing light on the TV and as dusk begins to fall I get up to draw the curtains and put on a couple of lamps. Alex sits deep in the sofa; his frame is large – he is a big man. He coughs repeatedly before lighting a cigarette and resumes staring at the TV. The room is awash with dancing light that cascade towards him. He sits resting like an immovable mountain. The light sparkles against his nose stud and his dark features lay hidden in the shadows.

The gospel song rises and falls to an ancient rhythm coursing through the hearts of the slaves. They have travelled so far and journeyed so hard. The breaking work cuts the flesh and evokes salted wounds full of puss and blood. The bodies may break, but there is something that cannot be broken. The song moves and weaves to an imagined future of freedom. It raises and falls and energises the suffering souls. From suffering to death and resurrection to life. The slaves move to a gentle rhythm that builds: it is building the foundation for a future time.

We listen to some Detroit Techno and the complex beats project out against a vivid soundscape. My mind breathes and my imagination begins to grow. The music reaches into me and fills me with energy and an envisioned world. The Detroit producers have made technology their own and I rest in deep thought listening to a timeless sound that evokes the past bridged to the future.

It fills me with funk: the ancient rhythm of the universe. Space takes on a new horizon and so much seems possible. This is the art of the African diaspora that pours into my soul and wakes me to the creative source. The diaspora soul has traversed space and time uniting the ancient world with the future: the timeless funk always existing beyond conception.

Alex stands heavily against the sound system and sifts through his records: he pulls out a beautiful vinyl record that sparkles with static energy as he removes it from the sleeve. With barely audible gestures he walks with fag in mouth back to the sofa. We sit and wait for the sound to draw out of the crackling needle.

"Yeah man." Alex says quietly with an unhurried smile.

The beat breaks and the riffs build. James Brown's soulful tone is crisp gold against the realities of life. He speaks to both of us and builds the song into a crescendo that asserts I am James Brown. I am and this is my world. With powerful funk Brown drives the darkness out of town. The refined musicianship of the band rests delicately with our minds and we feel empowered to live and breathe.
Alex closes his eyes and wearily covers them with his hands. He is heavy with the weight of the world. The distant figure of the psychiatrist circles in the distance seemingly waiting for his prey. Alex drifts into a dream world and places his half smoked cigarette in the ashtray to burn out. Awash with the painful memories of the psychiatrist's prison, Alex goes deep into himself; he finds solace and a universal prayer that evokes a longing for eternal life.

He expands his mind reaching out to the universe seeing countless mythical tales and other worlds. Riding the rhythm he rides the boat through the forest. The forest is timeless: it doesn't belong to any time or place – the warriors reveal themselves at the water's edge with bows held tight and silver knives at their sides. Their faces are painted and they wear maroon red cloth. They are perfectly still and allow themselves to be seen by Alex. Their beautiful features stare out at the river and they seem to speak to Alex without making a sound. Alex opens his eyes and looks down at the long ash trail at the end of his burnt out cigarette. He looks over to me and then with a look of recognition he sits back gently and rubs his face.

For the psychiatrist, dreams are empty of meaning and the behaviour of the insane has no value; the dreamer dreams of an imagined world and wakes to the callous specious gaze of the white devil. The overseer holds whip in hand and feeds the leather through his hard skin. The tobacco plants orchestrate a quiet whisper against the warm breeze. With hands covered in dirt and stained with blood, the slave pulls at the tough earth.

In the painful moments that his body endures his mind drifts into a timeless horizon. Out of time and space there is a future that is his to make. He works and works – always thinking of the Promised Land. The rhythm and the beat: the yearnings of the soul to overcome suffering and resurrect into a new life. Coltrane holds the sax and carves the most majestic sound. At times it jars against the ear as he fearsomely searches for the hidden rhythms. He breaks down the conventions and crafts new horizons offering a glimpse of what can be. He builds and then deconstructs and then rebuilds with new vigour.

Coltrane took refuge in heroin that was required to escape the prison bars of the Western psyche. He was a pioneer breaking down conventions; he sought the deeper mystical side of reality. The heroin succoured the troubled soul that had endured so much. Drugs have played their role in history. The ecstasy fuelled nights of dance music were needed to escape the ordinary and dance to a new vision.

For Alex, marijuana has been his refuge – that allows his mind to break away from the constraints of the world. He breathes the smoke and awakens the deeper parts of his mind that he may think freely and re-discover the spiritual journey that he is on. Coltrane was right on the edge and so is Alex. They are pioneers carving a new landscape for their people. This new landscape offers respite for the diaspora and in turn offers a vision to me and the rest of the world; that we might unite as a people and feed the soundscape into an enlightened society.

There is still darkness in the room. Alex sits impervious to his surroundings. Cold air sifts through beneath the front door and the windows creak to the gusts of smog outside. Where is there safety? There is only safety within the mind and we sit there together upright and proud; we observe the swirling rise of ghostly apparitions. Do ghosts exist? They exist in a sense; they arise from the thoughts of others that wish to do harm.

The haters pant and breathe salaciously, blanketed by the dark and they plot ways to feed their scaled reptilian bodies. There is something about the intent of mind that affects the environment. The rain pours down in the dark winter evening; faces are covered against the elements and the drone of mechanisation scours through the streets. The good walk the pathways hidden from view carefully making their steps across the hazardous terrain. The bad drift among the crowds and with piercing eyes they seek their dues. A cut to the throat and bullets in the gut – the haters hate and hate.

London is a dangerous city and Alex has traversed the concrete jungle swerving from danger and facing the fire with grace. From this life of tough realities he has developed a remarkable understanding of style – the power of funk to overcome the dark. He wears his cap tight and covers his eyes from view. He walks with confidence and agility; tight hooded jacket pulled down to his waist with deep blue denim jeans and futuristic footwear.

Life is a dance and he moves through the night in the groove holding tight to the funk. His jewellery is a hard deep gold and with step in sync he heads to the club. It's a scene built with many people and Alex is the rock that everything passes through. He's a communicator and brings people together with good vibes: the selector plays and the dancers dance. The radio waves cackle with messages and shouts to all in the game – and the message of the music funks up the air with jazzed up soundwaves. Shout out to the one like…big thanks to the mighty…keep it tight.

Getting in tune with the groove: you may think it is just a sound but it is more than that – it is a calling to the spiritual warriors to gather. The women fire up the vibe with tight fitting dancewear and gleaming jewellery that spreads out lasers across the dancefloor. The girls dance deep in the sound and send out power that changes the world. With his cap covering his eyes, Alex locks into the sound system and breaks some sweat. The beat drives and the heat rises – an ancient dance that is timeless bridging the past with the future.

Away from the haters the dancefloor is locked – no one can break in. The vibe transcends and a journey unfolds. My mind unwinds and my limbs loosen. The dance is like a meditation as I begin to feel free again and breathe in the heat. The soulful vibe of Drum n Bass is some kind of junk funk from the streets that touches some ancient rhythm and together we pick up the energy and soul to dream of a destined future. The rhythm breaks down the conventions of the world and lifts up our spirits such that nothing seems impossible.

The groove; the groove is like a flowing river that carves its own path – a future bound destiny through space. The haters dress up like they know the funk. They dress real cool and wear the hard gold metal. But there's something they just don't get. The gangsters stand at the edge of the dancefloor. An air of danger surrounds them and people keep out their way. The rhythm pushes and the beats break but the haters just stand there hidden in the shadows save for the glow of smokes.

The early days were raw man – the atmosphere was edgy but the selector kept his head. Alex knew who was in the club but he kept to the business of the sound and kept the funk in his veins. You gotta be tight – you gotta know who to trust – who's gonna watch ya back. The atmosphere is hot and heavy but the music drives.

So we sit there and Alex has an expectant eye on the danger that approaches. The haters move like shadows and where fear resides they take their due. You see, Alex is trying to keep his head but everything he does is demonised by the psychiatrist. His bursts of anger and his dream-like visions are deemed to be mental illness: so here he is keeping his head against the gangsters but he also has to contend with the soul crushing psychiatrist. The haters like this – it gives them fuel and a means to haunt Alex.

The black cold air creeps through the doors and nearby there is shouting and doors slamming. There is discontent in the atmosphere. The haters swirl through the smog picking at the broken minds in their path. Drug dens are like that. They are full of fear and the environment is thickly evil. The haters move in and weave a paranoid atmosphere. There is no laughter but cackles of filthy minds that reach with black stained fingers for the pipe. The hater intimidates and takes. He is dangerous because he feeds of the evil air and evokes a paranoid climate wherever he goes. Now, when you're trying to face up to these guys and you're also dealing with the psychiatrist – it is seriously tricky. But the soul survivor prevails.

We just sit there in silence. The weather turns bitter. The flat is cold; but we just sit there. It is a strange thing: the ghosts that travel on the bitter breeze. It seems to infiltrate the minds of everyone that breathes it in. The community psychiatric nurse pays a visit to Alex. We know what to expect; that they will be a weak-willed person following orders. The nurse peers blankly into Alex's mind and sees nothing but his own reflection: he licks his lips and opines that Alex continue to settle in the flat. Alex keeps still and quiet. This nurse may be a feeble creature but there is a poorly veiled threat beneath the surface. With a quick quizzical look at me the nurse finds his way out. Alex is unmoved and lights a cigarette to blow away the tepid energy. We sit and await the night.

The walls clatter with black claws crawling amidst the shadows; the TV blasts out cross-eyed politicians leading the country to nowhere. And we wait. The muffled groan of the traffic is unsettling as the filthy vapour of ill-intent moves through the city. To the psychiatrist this kind of perception is delusional and with forced treatment the patient is intoxicated with psychiatric poisons.

But evil is insidious and laughs at the voiceless hero besieged by the state oppressors. Evil rises in the clinical setting and in the hospital whispering guidance into the psychiatrist's mind. How can he say there is evil? The whispers slither, how can he call me such names? The doctor heeds the whispered advice and forces Alex to give in. But his mind and will cannot be broken.

Not all gangsters are evil; of course not. For many the only option is to fall into the shadows. In some ways Alex is a pioneer offering a new path. The consequence of history is such that many good men find themselves in bad company. The transition from suffering to a place in society is long and hard. The complexity of the African mind is such that it is vilified and demonised at every turn. The psychiatrist is the greatest enemy of the black man fighting his way up from the streets. There are times when you need to be a little crazy.

Someone who has risen through the streets knows evil all too well and the middle class white doctor simply has no understanding of how darkness works. Darkness is full of tricks and deceit. It will walk with you and offer a kind of power; but reacts foully when rejected. It is so hard to break away from because there is nowhere to break away to. For the soul rebel, there is only a frightening path – a high peak traverse full of risk between the underworld and the violence of the state.

The black man is on his own trying to understand his own mind within a hostile world that will demonise him at a pinch. This is why the music is so great –it is borne from the high peaks – from the true taste of reality. And it is through the sound that a new path is forged.

Alex rests with his eyes closed and with his proud demeanour sitting behind the light of the lamp; he raises his chest out before imagining. This is the mind – the power to imagine. But there is more to it than that – the imagination has the power to create. James Brown created James Brown and Alex allows his mind to discover a freedom that can be brought into this world.

The forest rustles with a cool breeze and his mind is invigorated. The surface of the river reflects the night sky and the moon stands as witness to the travelling seeker. He closes his eyes tightly and moves with the water. There is a rhythm to the elemental flow that is full of a thousand stories.

Alex's mind reverberates gently with the movement and he allows his mind to be massaged by the infinite waves of outer space. The river moves but his mind is still. The pulsating repetition of waves enters his body like a thousand shafts of light. They lighten his burden and fill him with the subtle language of nature. The rhythm and the flow: his body is illuminated and the boat rides a steady course in harmony with the river.

The medicine continues to make him lethargic and heavy; Alex breathes the smoke of a cigarette and tells me of his discomfort. He takes the drugs to keep the psychiatrist off his back but he knows the drugs are harming him. They are another brick in the wall – another obstacle to be overcome. The darkness plays tricks with the mind and flows in his veins with the medicine. If he were to tell the doctor this he would just be given more drugs and the darkness will then penetrate more deeply. He smokes his cigarettes and rests in his deeper mind which is impenetrable.

The soul. Soul power. Within his imagination there is a subtle frame of consciousness that gives rise to clear thought. Deep in his mind he perceives the creative source. The warriors stand on the edge of the river. They are calm, peaceful, and perfectly poised. Their movements glide effortlessly and they pull Alex closer to them. They come into clearer view and they smile warmly. Their eyes seem to be full of the stars.

Alex opens his eyes and with his cigarette gritted between his teeth he looks at me. The room is dimly lit by a single lamp and the rain taps invisibly against the windows. The atmosphere is damp. Again the cold night breeze seems to bring piercing voices in to the room; they circle us and cajole us to break. Alex stares outwardly still biting his cigarette. The night carries the icy whispers that move in and out of perception threatening the false safety of the physical world. We do not react; we are warriors observing our enemy unmoved and unafraid.

The atmosphere is heavy with the ill-intent from outside. Collectively the world seems to move like a viper's nest waiting to catch the soul rebel. The rebel seeks to break free and cut down the creeping roots of darkness. My love for Alex is such because he knows this state of existence all too well. This is the narrative of the black man from slavery to victory. The smiling face of the psychiatric nurse pretends to help but he only serves to further disempower Alex and gently weaves the chains around his neck with sinister gentleness.

Rage is the instinct of the heart that reacts to injustice – it is the language of the voiceless who know no other way. The mind is fragile and sensitive to the trickery of others; but when rage is the only expression it only serves to tighten the noose. The psychiatrist is cold and saps the air of energy. Alex feels that he can't breathe. He is filled with rage and his hollow voice ignites a deep anxiety in him. The psychiatrist crushes the spirit; and when the mind before him lays shattered he imposes his will on the patient. He tells Alex that his mentally ill – that his mind is false – that his thoughts are false. He disempowers Alex who sits silent in rage suffocated by the ever tightening rope.

The music that comes from this experience is the purest and richest expression of the soul. Amidst the horrors of experience a seed of beauty enters the world and slowly takes root. The psychiatrist licks his lips and salivates for his next flesh. He steals the life energy from his patients and holds power like that of a dictator based on fear. The soul rebel sits tied in chains; his body scorched and beaten. The taste of blood-filled sweat is all too familiar. The feeling of the hard dry soil is all too well known.

The mosaic that is the future world is filled with colours from every corner of the globe. The suffering has been terrible but through the bonds of friendship a new society takes shape. The majestic figure of Alex is muscular and fearsome. He sits like a bronzed figure with sight beyond the mundane and has visions of colour with vibrant creative possibilities. When I look at him I see an ancient warrior that is timeless in aspect and appears in this world but not of it.

Alex is a bodhisattva – a spiritual warrior that traverses space and time with a compassionate will. In his being lies the whole history of the African psyche that is rich in spiritual heritage and full of an imagination of what can be. Alex smiles – he is at times a frightening figure like a mighty warrior amidst battle – but he is full of warmth and gentleness. He moves his heavy limbs towards

the sound system and pulls out the album Cosmic Funk and
Spiritual Sounds by Lonnie Liston Smith.

The music is medicine to the soul and we sit together riding
the contours of imagination and space. Alex has come through
so much suffering but through it all he just seems to become
more handsome, bolder, and stronger. Life is like a dance – in
India there is a god, Shiva, who is lord of the dance. Throughout
ancient societies there has always been a culture of dance and
transcendence.

The psychiatrist may dominate the modern world but it is we who
stand on thousands of years of history. Like an ancient medicine
man with a staff in his hand and coloured threads in his hair;
Afrika Bambatta wears mirrored futuristic shades and says Dance
Sucker. It is the music that brings people together and it has the
power to change the world as a gift for everyone.

Alex throws the psychiatric drugs in the bin and stands up tall
scratching the back of his head. He gets changed into some fresh
clothes. He wears an electric blue fine cotton t-shirt and deep
coloured denim jeans. He pulls his cap tight and ties up the laces
of his dark blue trainers. He wants to break free; he polishes his
decks and sound system before blowing the dust off an old-school
House record. It brings back memories of the early days when
things were free and all there was to do was dance.

The beats breathe out from the speakers and bounce against the walls. The bass vibrates pushing out deep waves of air. There is no sight of the psychiatric ward as we laugh and smoke to the music. The air is crisp and the traffic outside seems to hum to a vibrant rhythm. The winter sun breaks out and there is a blue sky amidst the scarves of wrapped up shoppers and the world outside.

"I think it's time to go out," he tells me.

Chapter 3

The Technics rest on a strong black metal frame – the silver surface of the 1200s glint against the sunlight and the needle cuts the groove on the vinyl. Alex stands at the decks with his head tilted to one side listening into the headphones. The gold of his rings flash as he pulls the fader and his metal bracelet hangs loosely. He manipulates the sound and sets forth broken beats. He wears a strong red sweater with a hood and moves in tune to the sound. He's rolling out some liquid funk Drum n Bass which lightens the air and makes us feel good.

The soulful vocals ride the melody and the rolling breaks energise. There's a good vibe around at the moment and for a few days we enjoy the positive feelings. There are no nutters banging at the door and the haters seem to be far away. This is a time to renew our spirits and strengthen our resolve. The traffic pours through the London streets and crowds of people dart from one destination to another.

Alex walks with a proud gait as we make our way to the pub.

The pretty barmaid smiles as we enter; she wears a tight t-shirt that shows her physique. There's something about a pretty girl that just makes you feel better.

"What you 'avin mate?" I ask Alex.

"Fuck. Dunno. I'll have what you're having. Are you on the Guinness?"
"Yeah. I think so."

"Alright I'll have the same. You know beer's not my thing but 'ere we go."

Alex looks round the pub and I sense he feels a bit of an outsider. It's the daytime so it is not too busy. There's a table next to the fire place which I gesture to Alex to grab. We sit down; it's an old fashioned London pub and the interior has kept to the original style. The air is fresh outside and the sky is blue with a crisp winter's bite. The fire gives out a gracious warmth and we sit with our pints like two old men.

"Fuck's sake." Alex mutters. "Where have you brought me?"

I laugh and say "cheers" as I gulp the Guinness. We sit for a few minutes without talking and we each seem to be lost in our thoughts.

"Why d'you white boys drink so much?"

"Dunno man; I guess it's the culture."

"Yeah."

Alex draws the pint glass to his mouth and takes a sceptical sip. Drafts of cold air wash towards us every time the door opens with people entering and leaving. The smell of the burning wood in the fireplace offers a soothing respite against the winter breeze. It'd be nice to have a fag but the fucking health police have banned that. Before making our way outside to smoke, we sit for a few moments watching the different faces arrive at the bar. The pub has always been a place of refuge for the Englishman. There is something about beer that warms the heart and settles the mind. Pubs have existed for hundreds of years in British culture through many wars and many generations.

"Shall we get some food?" I ask Alex.

"Yeah man. I'm starvin'."

I call over to the pretty barmaid and we order a couple of steaks. She is so pleasing to the eye and lifts both our spirits.

"Gotta get me a bird man. My balls are bursting." Alex looks towards the girl who is walking back to the bar and we both enjoy the view of the nice soft arse.

"Yeah man. I hear what you're saying." I take a gulp of the Guinness and slam it down. "Another one?"

"For fuck's sake white boy! I've still got half to go."

"Alright man!"

I laugh and head up to the bar for another one. Looking over to Alex, I see him staring in to the fire. His large frame fills the chair – but he doesn't look out of place. And he gives no sense of feeling out of place. He is a Londoner; as cockney as the Artful Dodger. His mind is street-wise and he fearlessly takes his sharp wit wherever he goes.

There is something about the tradition of the pub that perhaps became stuck in time. It is certainly a beautiful part of our culture – but did a homogenous Anglo-Saxon culture reach its peak? Was there any further to go? It is a given that our finest hour was defeating the Nazis: but what happened to us after this? The Empire receded and degeneracy seemed to creep in to the culture. I can't help feel that the African soul is perhaps needed to offer something new to these islands.

I mean, could you imagine a world without funk? The grey skies and bland food of yesteryear are perhaps best left in the past. At first sight Alex makes for a frightening figure. He is big, muscular, and his dark skin to the Victorian mind would have seemed otherworldly. In some sense the Empire spread out to the world and now the world has come to Britain. I am thankful for that. There is something about the African mind that evokes a radical change in our perception of the world.

I think the mechanised world view of industrialisation killed off the spiritual and imaginative side of the Anglo-Saxon psyche. Alex in his upfront way offers a wake-up call to getting back in touch with the deeper rhythms of life. For me that is what the music is all about. I wonder if perhaps we are at the beginning of something – of the birth of a new people that will resonate in myth for hundreds of years to come.

"Yo man." Alex signals to me. "I'm going out for a fag." The cold breeze of the winter's day blasts into the pub as Alex opens the door. The London streets hum in a familiar tone. The barmaid smiles.

For the moment Alex's records are scattered in cardboard boxes in an unorganised fashion. Having set some shelving up, he goes about organising them. He must have several thousand records with everything from Jazz, Soul, and Reggae to Detroit Techno. It seems the whole history of black music since the early 20th century is in these boxes. He carefully pulls out the records and places them neatly on the wooden shelves. The records are ordered carefully in different genres and eras.

It's an amazing thing seeing all these records and the very real potential sound that exists in them. As we pull them out I take a moment to look at the wonderful artwork and photographs on the sleeves. There are classic Jazz records, Blues, Funk, and Soul. Miles Davis stares out from the sleeve behind the coolest shades; and there's a Parliament Funkadelic album with multi-coloured psychedelic art.

Alex stands on the shoulders of giants; he is the heir to the sound and the lineage of funk travels through history right up to the tip of the Technics needle. With a fag in his mouth Alex talks through the smoke and tells me to check out a classic Juan Atkins track. He reaches up to place the record on the turntable and releases the crackling static.

"This is one of the earliest Techno tracks." He tells me. "Juan Atkins: the originator of Detroit Techno. The beat is raw man."

The early electronic sound from the mid-eighties breathes out the speakers and I hear the pioneering sound of what was to influence the next twenty years of dance music.

"The Detroit sound is special man. These guys developed a whole new futuristic vibe. But you know what man." He reaches for another record before continuing. "Europe played its part in this music. Check this out: Kraftwerk. This is what inspired the Detroit boys."

It fascinates me that black guys from the US were so inspired by this German outfit. Somehow the African psyche was drawn to this synthesised music being created by the Germanic soul. It seems so implausible, but deep in northern Europe the metallic computerised music of Kraftwerk touched the minds of the Detroit artists.

The electronic music coming out of the States was soon to reach the shores of the UK and it was in the late eighties that Alex first heard Acid House in the record shop. He tells me that when he heard it; that was it – he was hooked. He was there at the beginning of the dance scene and rode the wave through the nineties. I look eagerly through his collection for early 90s House and the burgeoning Jungle music of the mid-90s. Alex was thick in the Jungle sound and he pulls out rare white labels and dub-plates smiling at the memories they invoke.

"There's some gangster shit right there." He jokes. "They were tough beats for a tough crowd man; a proper London sound." He rubs his face and says quietly, "yeah man…just for you London."

We spend several hours sorting out the records and then sit down to have a brew. Alex rests deep back in the sofa and blows cigarette smoke up towards the ceiling. The records set a framework to the room and give out a kind of reassuring energy. There stacked in those shelves is a history of sound that has changed the world.

Despite a good few days, Alex appears weary. The flat is quite cold as winter draws in. There is a solemnity to the air and we both wonder what the next few weeks will bring. Alex has been off his medication for a couple of weeks now but we both know that the battle with the state is not over yet. All those artists stacked in the shelves battled with authority. I think of Bob Marley's album Confrontation where he is depicted as St George slaying a dragon. That's the way it is. This music is borne from struggle. Babylon still casts a shadow over our lives.

The rain pours down and cars splash through the drenched roads. The thick red trail of tail lights are like a snaking creature moving through the city. The glare from car headlights blind us as we walk down the street. It is dark and we tread carefully through the sodden city to our destination. We wear thick dark jackets with hoods up and beneath the high buildings we dance through the city to a rough beat. We are future bound and move in sync with the universe. The funk empowers our movements and we stride the planet with creative intent.

The city is like a sleeping beast. It lies still but breathes heavily. It's when times are good that you have to be most aware of what the city might throw up in your path. The haters are out there riding the underbelly of the town. The underworld writhes beneath the streetlights and hidden minds creep through the alleyways intent on bad deeds. Hands meet in dark corners and wrapped packages are exchanged.

Dirty money is taken and blades glint against the dull yellow light. The haters cover their faces and all that remains are piercing eyes that stare cold hard. They mirror visions of a different life that exists in the cracks and dark places of society. They move without sound and seem invisible to the eye. They have no conscience and cut flesh without hesitation.

Alex sits upright and proud on the sofa but he is not relaxed. The wind and rain hitting the windows seem to bring messages of dark intent. The flat is dimly lit and Alex sits motionless. His gold jewellery is hard against the weak light; smoke rises from the cigarette in the ashtray. The psychiatrist tells Alex that he is paranoid – that his fears are delusional. This plays into the haters' hands; they love it that Alex battles the state. The dark creeps; it is insidious and unseen. The psychiatrist waits with his sharp blade and the haters stare with red eyes.

The night is thick with the scent of trouble – the roads seem to incite a deadly hum as the weather gets worse. Alex sits unmoved – he rests deep in the shadows and closes his eyes. He enters a timeless zone and rests his mind in the vastness of space. The subtle vibration of the music drifts into his consciousness and the dub sound awakes him to the mind state of the spiritual warrior. He rests deeply in the sound. The physical world breaks apart and he grows in stature. The hidden riddim moves through his veins and love fills his heart. The night passes intense with danger but Alex rides it and opens his eyes to the morning sun.

The landscape rises with the sun and the world sets about the business of the day. The Eton educated suits stand with their pointy noses at the despatch box. The chamber echoes with the tired arguments of left versus right – and the issues of the day fill the headlines and the news. Yet another boy murdered. London is sick with deprived areas where disease is rife. There are places where the angels fear to tread. The tower blocks of the city's council estates rot with the poison of drugs and violence.

Alex knows this world all too well – for him it was the music that offered a way out. The music seemed to create its own path out of the ghetto. The story of the black man whether in the US or London is one of rising from the ashes. Bob Marley sang of the concrete jungle and the funk bands built a rhythm that broke free.

Why is it that the African diaspora still face such hardship? There seems to be a disconnection between the boy from the ghetto and the high walls of Westminster. The psychiatric ward is full of broken minds that lie vulnerable to the psychiatrist's brutality. It is claimed they are mentally ill; but is not the truth that their minds offer a language that is misunderstood by psychiatry? That the craven science of materialism is a brutal administer of psychiatric poison.

Ours is a culture two thousand years old but how old is that of Africa? It seems the only knowledge of his African heritage comes through his dreams and of course the music. For Alex he can hear his African roots in the horn of Coltrane and the dub pressure of roots Reggae. That all physical memory can be removed but the past still exists in the psyche and from the earliest songs on the plantations the ancient rhythm builds into new life.

A sound and a vibration come out of the speakers that are otherworldly; the fine lines break through the air and the carved structures frame the vision. I rest in the sound and dream of a future. The tired old ways creak and the walls begin to fall as a spectrum of colour and the vastness of a new world break through.

The beat breaks and we burst into life. Alex throws me a cigarette and we head out into town. The vibe is purposeful and we walk down the stairs into the bass filled room. Faces shift in and out of the strobe light as we make our way to the bar. The sound is heavy and the night is well into the early hours. The conventional disappears and we enter the soundscape of the dancefloor. The rhythm of the music sends out cosmic waves throughout the world and it is here that the future is created. The waves push up out of the underground and into the Victorian architecture of London; they break through the city walls and funk up Buckingham Palace. The dancers move against the lights and creative expression blasts to the sound.

In the early hours twilight offers a glimpse into a timeless zone; as the world sleeps and the working day is yet to begin. We rest in the low light of the living room listening to some ambient sounds. Cigarette smoke fills the air and we bathe our minds in those primordial moments before the city creaks into life. I think of my own history and my own dreams. The music expands the mind and I blow smoke into the low light. Where is my place in this world?

I am something of an outsider and I think this is why the music appeals to me so much. I am searching for my home. I am a traditionalist at heart but I feel so far away from the establishment. Funnily enough I do identify with Kate who I think I have a similar background to; the Royal family married into the middle class and I think this is a great move. I do feel that the next step should be an ethnic minority. The English are not a race: we are a people.

England never had a revolution and as such much of the traditional framework of society still exists: the Monarchy, the Church, Parliament. Although I believe the institutions are still very relevant I do feel that something is missing. The dominant mode of knowledge is scientific – what we can see. But can science see the mind? The psychiatrist regards Alex's behaviour as dysfunctional and as mental illness; but is he not missing something? The language of the soul that speaks of deeper things.

Alex rides the threshold; the beat is his refuge – the music is his sanctuary. He wears bold colours and walks upbeat through life – he is a seeker and strives for meaning. This alien society has been a battlefield for the West Indian – at every turn they have been demonised and misunderstood. But their heroics in adversity are such that they have inspired me. The music offers a different vision of life. The scientific mind promotes function and utility above all – it tells us there is no deeper meaning to life. But the colour and the funk always break through.

Alex drifts into a dream. The river continues on its long journey through space. The river widens and the boat seems to grow in stature. The stars break out in the night sky and the warrior stares up at them navigating his path. There is a powerful silence that speaks of fullness rather than emptiness. The warrior does not feel alone but feels the whole presence of nature. The boat makes steady progress breaking through the gentle waves. The water is deep and the surface reflects and refracts the light of the night sky.

The boat moves through darkness but there is no sense of fear. Tall thick trees appear that stretch their branches over the river offering a royal arch for the approaching boat. Alex is going deep into his mind: into his psyche. In the psyche nothing is forgotten – all memory remains. A warrior with a bow appears and majestically fires an arrow into the sky. The rhythm builds and a light sound of drums transform the landscape into a vortex of light and sound.

The light of the day rises and pushes through the closed curtains offering a luminous glow to the living room. The ashtray lies overflowing with cigarette butts but the flat remains clean and tidy. The dub pressure styles out of the speakers and a deep rhythmic bass washes through the room. Alex opens the window and the sound of mechanised life comes in with cold gusts of wind.

"So another day begins." He says.

"Yeah man. Another day." I reply.

Alex is still a little overweight from the psychiatric drugs but he is starting to regain some energy and feel less lethargic. The day offers a grey and damp air. It is quite cold and Alex goes round the flat turning on a few electric heaters. Money is tight and he tries not to keep them on for too long. The streets of London are abuzz with the sound of cars splashing through puddles and lorries heavily accelerating. The country and the world are in a strange place at the moment. There is so much change and unsettling wars abroad.

It seems to me that Alex is a timeless warrior from another age. He is no fool for the tricks and false friendship that evil offers. Evil is a strong word; but there is no doubt to our minds that it thrives and squirms through the London concrete. The haters sit tight and count filthy piles of cash. There seems to be a climate at the moment in which the haters thrive. There is so much paranoia and fear around: the very conditions that bad people thrive in.

There are many broken minds in London. Some are casualties of the drug-fuelled nineties; others just crack against the trap of poverty and no opportunity. It's quite something to see the world of someone diagnosed with paranoid schizophrenia. They are hidden away in run-down council flats; they are usually overweight from the medicine; and they live an isolated existence with only the TV as comfort. It is in these dark recesses of the city that evil squalors.

The psychiatric patient is left alone in a confused whirl of hallucinations unable to decipher the unreal from the real. The psychiatric nurse pays occasional visits and the psychiatrist just prescribes stronger drugs. It is testament to Alex's strength of mind that he has not ended up like this. It saddens me that many of these psychiatric patients are of West Indian descent. It seems that the white man brought these men to the West and left them to rot in the ghetto. Their wild and indiscernible psychotic symptoms are offered no compassion but laced with powerful anti-psychotic medicine.

But just take a minute and you will discover meaning to be deciphered. Many of the psychotic expressions have a religious flavour. I think in the height of paranoia and fear the mind reaches to express a deeper yearning. The psychiatrist dismisses these expressions of the mind as meaningless and insane.

One aspect of the African mind that I really like is the resolute belief in spirituality. It seems to me that the slavery ships of the West were symbols of scientific reason that held a superiority complex against nature. The wild eyed African whose eyes were full of the stars of the night sky and whose mind was so tuned in with the natural world was deemed subhuman. The specious scientist peered at these creatures and sought to imprison their souls. Bob Marley sings of the Soul Captive.

The warrior spirit of Alex is held captive in the hull of the ship. But is he not a hero who will revolutionise the West? The bonds of reason are tight and the mechanics of the Western world whir and clunk; industry consumes and builds. But there is something missing. Poverty fills the London streets of the 1950s and ragged children play with dirt. There is no colour but greyness and damp wastelands. In the midst of this era Little Richard strummed his guitar and multi-coloured light beams entered the world. Funk broke through.

Riding on the coloured light beams is the dream of a future world. The shallow consciousness of science is fractured by a blinding light that comes from deep in the psyche and dreams of creative expression and an eternal dance. Frodo throws the ring into the fire and Mordor collapses; the soul rebel lights his flame and Babylon falls.

The club offers a refuge for the soul captive; the music frees the mind from the constraints of the day and the beats drive. There is a scene of like-minds who make their way to the club following a day of monotonous work. The freaks come out at night. I often think of the US cities in the seventies when the freaks would come out at dark. This is when the psyche is free to reveal and express itself. The daylight seems to imprison the mind, but the night with the glow of the moon seems to release the hidden side of consciousness.

It was in the tough urban settings full of poverty and danger that Funk was born. In the night there is freedom but there is also danger – the soul captive has an intimate knowledge of danger.

On the dark side of the moon souls weave a path through the vipers and dance to the beat. People gather and check out the new sounds; the girls dance and flash their jewellery. The streets are empty save for the night people: we walk purposefully with jackets tight and a cutting vibe. The shadows move back and forth from the dark corners. A ghetto soldier sits hidden in his car with only the whites of his eyes showing. Warfare stalks the silent wet roads. Cars drive slowly with sinister intent and we step cleanly avoiding the gaze.

The night grows deeper and the imagination dreams. There is a new world and a new horizon. Time is relative – the past and the future are immutable. Far in the forest of the mind a rhythm unfolds and countless myths shine out from the stars. With a face painted blood-red save for dark circles around the eyes; the dancer sticks out his tongue which is pierced with a metal bar. His eyes are wild with otherworldly visions. The rhythm rises as the dancers step hard with their legs and raise their heads upwards. The forest vibrates with cosmic energy and seems to enter a timeless zone.

This is a dance of the wakeful dream that moves and breathes through the dancers. The painted faces cry out furious spells and the fire glows against their skin spitting flames into the air. This dance is a mandala that rests in the psyche. It is absolute and unbreakable: like an erupting volcano it forms a future landscape.

Unseen the haters set their blades on the table and they talk among themselves. There is a thickly intimidating atmosphere.

Telephones are full with numbers and trade is made with other haters around the city. The wasteland of the ghetto is covered in litter and walkways are desolate haunted by sharp knives and bestial force. No authority has the strength to heal these streets: the police leave them to kill themselves.

The white middle classes go about their lives either in ignorance or just not wanting to know. There goes another one: another broken mind taken to the psychiatric ward. The psychiatrist wrenches the vulnerable mind to and fro and administers the poison. The landscape is dry and lifeless; the hater sells his shit and the shadows walk the night with firearm at the ready. This is no place for heroes. It reeks of infection and untouchable disease.

Alex stands at his turntables and releases the record. Waves of synth push out and the broken beats build the pressure.

"So how we gonna change this planet man?" Alex asks.

"I think the answer lies in understanding the mind." I reply.

"The mind." Alex repeats quietly. "Yeah man there is so much potential in the mind. As Ferris Bueller says if you put your mind to it you're capable of anything."

"Isn't that sampled on an LTJ Bukem track?"

"It was a tune that he used to play back in the day. I loved that sound back then – intelligent Drum n Bass. But it's true you know bro; the answer is in the mind."

Alex pulls out a couple of records and puts some old 90s Drum n Bass on. Some great tunes were made back then: the synth washes through the room and the upbeat melody breaks with the fast tempo beats. Hearing this sound again reminds me of the cool intelligent funk that came out of Hip-Hop bands like Digable Planets and De La Soul. It was all about cool funky dreads and colourful clothes. Good vibes.

Very often the cooler funk vibe was overshadowed by the harder sound of gangster Rap and hard aggressive Drum n Bass. I'm not against the harder sound but I do feel the power of the intelligent vibe is often overlooked. DJs like Bukem and Fabio would build cool flowing beats into their sets that made everyone feel good and when I listen to this music it is like medicine – it rids the environment of haters.

In this soulful sound there was a calling to imagine a future and dance to the space funk. Its music you can sit to and go deep into the imagination and thought. It lifts our energy and gets us thinking ways of funking up the planet.

"You know," Alex talks above the music, "I'm not religious but I am spiritual. I don't know about God or life after death; but I believe in this life and what can be achieved."

"Yeah I hear what you're saying." I light up a cigarette and blowing smoke in the air I get to thinking.

"All the best music is spiritual." Alex points at his record collection. "Right from Gospel to Jazz to Bob – they all took power from the spiritual. I like to think of the creative source you know, that in this life anything is possible."

"Yeah man. What I love about Coltrane is that he was a spiritual seeker and you know he searched beyond Christianity into India. India shares the same kind of improvisational approach to music. I think a lot of Western classical music is so stultified and wooden: but Coltrane saw in India this wonderful culture of spiritual searching through music. You know I still don't think the world recognises how great Coltrane was. He traversed space and time man. He created a sound that was universal that connected with the whole world."

"Yeah definitely. I understand what you're saying – and it was the African mind that imagined the world through sound."

"Yeah man. That's true. It was an African mind that orchestrated a vision of world unity."

The mandala begins to take shape and every corner of the world begins to offer something to a future landscape. Every language on earth can be found in London; but still it seems to me that the greatest music in the world comes from the African diaspora. The funked up lens of the African mind transforms the grey stilted atmosphere into colour and movement.

Of course, white folk can make great sound. I think of the punk music of the 70s that broke through the stale air of London; and bands like the Clash were among the first to recognise a kindred rebel spirit in the West Indians. The white working class were quick to appreciate the Rasta's beat. It must have been very tough in London in the 70s; the police were brutal in their approach to the West Indian community. But through it all the music lives and black music is now deeply ingrained in our culture. African roots: English heart. Alex speaks with a tough south London accent and laughs like an Englishman. We sit listening to the music; the vibe builds and we imagine.

The wind blows against the front door and a cold draft comes from the windows. The low light of winter evening takes hold and there is restless energy moving through the city. Cars drive slowly with dimmed headlights and pockets heavy with blades walk through the night. The bitter breeze seems to carry omens of bodies to be cut and knifed. Where's Jack the Ripper?

The ghetto calls out to the youth; no qualifications and no prospects. The glamour of the gangster way of life: of money, clothes, and BMWs. The kingpin has people around him who do his bidding – the reason they do it is that there is nowhere else where they feel they belong. The London air is thick with paranoid intensity. London is full of gangsters: but there is no single top dog who rules the streets.

At the bottom level there are the postcode gangs; just kids who have a totally distorted view of the world. Theirs is a world of knives, petty drug dealing, and sexual deviance. The latter is derived from a polluted understanding of sex from the internet: and this is just mainstream porn. Among the postcode gangs there is a deep misogyny and girls are routinely bullied into deprived sexual acts. This is part of the initiation and the payment for belonging. There is no moral framework and there is no authority that is capable of helping these kids. The ghettoization of deprived areas sinks ever deeper into a cesspit and is a sore that the metropolitan class can only ignore.

In the 90s even in the most deprived areas there was one thing that made its way into every council flat: Jungle music. To the authorities this drug-fuelled aggressive sound was anathema to them. It was a devil music and revolved around a drug culture. I must admit that I avoided the Jungle scene initially and kept to the Detroit Techno vibe – it wasn't until I heard Goldie's Timeless and the more melodic vibe of Bukem that I was sold to it.

Jungle was a music from the streets and it was a serious sound that gave rise to very talented producers and DJs: it was a way out. Jungle developed into Drum n Bass and for the last twenty years it has evolved into a masterful art form. So my point is: music is the way out. I am convinced that on those sink estates you will not only find talented footballers but there is also an untapped pool of brilliant musicians.

The Bellville three: Juan Atkins (the originator); Kevin Saunderson (the elevator); Derrick May (the innovator) stand amidst the ruins of Detroit but incredibly offer the world a vision of the future. The African mind is expressed through the machine and the most amazing art and sound are created. In London the mighty Fabio and Grooverider have guided Drum and Bass to become as solid as a diamond ready for the next generation.

The soul survivors – the renegades of funk – stand largely unnoticed by mainstream society but offer an important vision. The mind of the African diaspora breaks through the soundwaves: into the living room comes a timeless vision of the past uniting with the future. The funk breaks down conventions and offers an alternative conception and perception of the world. Amidst all this is the dance: the DJ releases the pressure onto the dancefloor and time falls away to creative expressions and colour.

Alex rests deep in the sofa and rubs his face intensely. It is late at night: far into the early hours where and when the mind can loosen the constraints of the world and think freely. There is a low light in the living room and Alex presents a distant figure as he sits back in himself. Although it is hard to see him there is a sense of a large man quietly contemplating – much like the ominous presence of a mountain covered by night.

It's all about the beats. Faced with the battles that confront him he rests deep in his mind. The night air is full of dark whispers and the silence of the streets belies a sinister intent. Although it is late we begin to talk.

"Do you believe in God man?" Alex asks me.

"That's not a straightforward question to answer." I reply. "I think it depends on what we mean by God. I think it is fair to say that I reject the concept of God as understood by the bible: that there is some kind of personified deity that has existed through history. But it's a complex issue. What's your view?"
"I believe in something you know. Call it the creative source or whatever: that there is a deeper mystery to life and that there is such a thing as truth."

"Yeah, I hear what you're saying. I think that's my view as well. The creative source. I like that."

We both sit without moving. We rest in our minds. With closed eyes a vision appears of the night sky reflected in water. The river flows towards the creative source. Africa wakes to a dream world and a community pull us towards them. In the night air there is a sense of rich green as the forest nears. Stars are scattered across the sky and the crescent moon shines gently.

There is a rhythm and a beat that evokes an understanding of the mysteries of reality – it speaks of both the past and the future. It heals our minds and energises us. The boat moves cutting through the silk water. Space appears as infinite and it seems anything is possible. There is a unifying force that whispers wisdom of a future world.

I look at Alex and he is sitting back in the sofa lost in thought. I get up and look around me; the night rain patters against the window. The flat is cold and I grab my jacket leaving Alex to dream and carry my own thoughts of where my path lies.

I am fascinated by the triple gem that is the Monarchy, the Church, and Parliament – these central institutions are the roots of power in the UK. It is true that British black people are underrepresented in these power bases. I can't help but feel that as relevant as the institutions still are, there is something missing. I feel we are dining out on the family silver – we still stand in the shadows of the Victorians. My view is that the homogenous landscape of Anglo-Saxon England reached its zenith in the Victorian and Edwardian eras: eventually the homogeny fractured and broke after two world wars.

The fifties called out to the Commonwealth to revitalise a thinning workforce. English society in the fifties was in some ways idyllic but it was also grey, lacking passion, and you might say dying. The West Indians brought their music and the Indians brought their spirituality. The rivers of the Empire that reached out to the world now laid open a road back to England. A central tenet of Christianity is the idea of proselytising and spreading its message as far and wide as possible. The Victorian Christian believed it a duty to Christianise and civilise the world. Whatever the wrongs of this; there is no denying that it was the seed for a globalised planet. To the grey sodden British Isles came the powerful cultures and minds of Africa and India.

The root of Christianity is compassion and this is the core message of many spiritual traditions not least the ancient world of Tibet. This is why Christianity is still very important: questions about God are secondary to the development of a compassionate mind. This is something that the rationalism of science cannot understand: it presumes that the mind cannot be perceived and therefore it does not exist. When I see these broken minds in the psychiatric ward I see disturbed minds that need healing.

Psychiatry does not heal because it does not have a concept of mind. Psychiatry only sees function and dysfunction – it presumes that dysfunctional behaviour requires fixing. This is utterly barbaric in my view. Yes, in the short term psychiatry may offer some respite to the symptoms but in the long term only a spiritual method of healing the mind can help. This is compassion. The mind responds to warmth, empathy, and love. There is also a certain denial in psychiatry about the reality of the world: that there is no danger out there. It is no good 'fixing' a paranoid mind by denying them the validity of their perceptions.

This is the calling: that all the peoples of the world contribute to the creation of a future planet. London is the capital of the future. Alex sits deep in his mind. His large figure rests motionless veiled by shadows. His gold jewellery shines out of the hidden corner and he talks slowly but with purpose. He knows the violence of the streets all too well. His mind is tuned to survival; he knows the taste of the filthy air.

The beats are his refuge and they empower a transcendent perception of the world. The beats roll rhythmically breaking the air and carve a path out of the darkness. He stands tall and very strong: the selector holds the vinyl and fades one sound into another. We wear tight fitting well-made clothes and embrace the styles of fashion. Women attract to brave minds and dance on the cutting edge drawing the warrior ever further into the threshold. Women incite a power that drives the beat harder and the selector cuts the tunes more finely.

"You know man," I say to Alex, "I wish they'd use an electric organ in Church. The tired old organ and the tired old hymns are just so dull. The electric organ could expand our minds with futuristic sounds."

"Yeah I kinda hear what you're saying." Alex stands with one ear in his headphones next to the decks.

"You see, imagination is the means by which the mind grows and develops. It is from the mind that the world is created. This world is the accumulation of the thoughts and imaginings from the past. You don't find yourself in life: you create yourself. I think this is what the music is all about."

"Yeah man. I hear that. Funk is about creating both yourself and a new world."

"Yeah definitely. Through the sounds and our imagination we

literally create a new reality. I think this is essentially what prayer is. It is using the mind's power to forge a new horizon."

The white man dreams of commerce and global power – that wealth will rain down on the West. The captured soul dreams of freedom and somehow breaking the chains that imprison him. Two dreams collide. The soundwaves break into our living rooms and radically influence the minds of the young.

The searching guitar of the Blues and the pristine horn of Jazz breaks through the speakers and revolutionises the West. This music carries tales of suffering and dreams of a future. It breaks the mould and fractures old certainties. It is the power of the mind and soul that re-imagines and re-creates a new horizon. Alex pulls back the vinyl with a scratch and releases it exploding the beat into the damp air.

I pull some books from my bookcase: Fichte, Hegel, Schelling. The period of German idealist philosophy is comparable with that of ancient Greece. You won't find many idealists in British philosophy departments these days; which is strange because I believe it to be the greatest of modern philosophy. The materialists dominate the academic world which is so removed from the ordinary world. They argue over minutia and texts that are impenetrable to the ordinary mind. The Oxbridge dons scowl at the inferior ordinary man and raise their noses based on some notion of intellectual superiority.

But they are sophists and if Socrates were alive today he would have a field day as a gadfly. Idealist philosophy is generally traced to the work of Plato who wrote of forms and ideals that exist beyond the conventional world. That beauty in this world reflects a more perfect idea in the spiritual world.

In Plato's parable of the cave it is the true philosopher (the true spiritual seeker) that steps away from the shadows and dares to see beauty in its perfect form. Beauty pervades our lives and we chase it like the ends of rainbows seeking our fortune and happiness; so often we are foiled by its elusiveness and find nothing.

Music aspires to beauty and undoubtedly the Western classical tradition has created many masterpieces; but this sound doesn't satisfy my soul. Dance music creates wild sounds that reach and push for endless new forms and it is here in the dance that conventions break down to reveal the horizon of perfect forms. The dancer tightens his space shoes and pulls his hooded jacket taut against the night. Bass pressure waves push out of the speakers and the dancefloor vibes to expressive steps.

There is something in this funk; something that is rising unexpectedly from an unseen source. The intellectuals and the scientists measure and analyse the bottom of the sea determined to measure the world and eventually the universe. Funk comes from within – the inner universe. It cannot be measured – but it is from the inner source that the world is created. The mythical warriors of Africa knew this – they knew how to connect with the stars and how to breathe in the energy of the universe.

The rhythm and the drums heightened consciousness and the medicine man could travel through time and space discovering new worlds. Reality is a network of jewels that rise and fall in unison to the breath of the universe. 'There' cannot exist without 'here'. On the surface the materialists repress the rising tide of the imagination; but theirs is a world failing because it is false. The rising imagination of the renegades of funk pushes and pushes until they break through into the ordinary and radicalise it into a new form.

Compassion is the very fabric of the mind –it is its essence. The purpose of religion is to cultivate a compassionate mind. That's it. Christ symbolises the perfection of mind – the very root of our psyches. Music helps cultivate this mind. It helps to transform the mind thereby lifting us up out of suffering. Reality is complex and mysterious and it is with music that we can traverse the fine lines of reality understanding its subtlety and vastness.

The synth of the Detroit sound washes through my living room and expands my mind. The sparkling sound imagines a horizon beyond the ordinary and the beats create a rhythmic pathway that guides the seeker. My mind becomes supple and I meditate on an infinite ocean of vibrancy and possibility.

The music inspires a friendship with others and it feels that I am energised by the life-filled universe. From this mind new ways of living are conceived and new technology invented. A whole new society and world takes shape. Parliament is about to get funked up. Monarchy is about to be funked up. The Church is going to be funked up. The planets align and the seekers hear the calling for a new age.

Chapter 4

Now well into the 21st century the music is better than ever. The early pioneers of the sound inspired a huge evolution in the technology. There is now no barrier from making whatever sound you want: the only restriction is that of the imagination. The rise of EDM has taken hold of US popular culture but for me it is soulless music. Even so the pioneers of the Detroit sound are still making their art be it beneath the recognition of mainstream society. Like the Drum and Bass scene in London, the pioneering producers and DJs have cultivated a culture that is really very strong.

EDM and mainstream music has no power to change the world; but the real musicians continue beneath the radar and I feel they have built something exceptional. Social commentators that I admire admonish the state of modern music but I just feel they have either overlooked or cannot see the brilliance of real dance music. There is something about the beats and the creative synth sounds that inspire my mind and imagination.

What I love about it is that it is a music that embraces technology and a vision of the future. There is no denying that this exquisite vision of the future has arisen in the African diaspora mind both in the US and here in the UK. It is sad to see growing issues around race in the US; but I have never sensed this with the Detroit artists.

Here in the UK I feel there are less tensions around race – go to any Drum and Bass night and there is almost no bad vibes with all races and backgrounds having a good time. This is testament to the guidance of the leading figures in the scene. The politicians talk the talk, but it is in the Drum n Bass clubs where the young are getting on with breaking down barriers and forming the future landscape.

Can deep thought and a serious vision of the world go hand in hand with dance music? Certainly I think the Detroit artists regard their work as having a serious point to make. One of my favourite House tracks is The Wanderer by Romanthony; I feel something of an outsider in the world and this tune really touched me. The voice on the track says that it is the system that makes you a wanderer and I really identify with this. I think it has been the system that has caused people of African descent in the US and the UK to feel like outsiders and wanderers.

Through the most difficult times in my life one of the constants has been the music. Adrift on desolate waters it was the sound of Fabio & Grooverider on the radio late at night that lifted my spirits. I owe something to this sound. You know a music is real when it speaks to you in the darkest moments. From Gospel, Blues, Jazz, Soul to Funk; this music has been created by people experiencing the true realities of life. This music is borne from the high peaks of soul searchers seeking their higher ground. While EDM takes over the charts, the real artists are deep underground ever refining their art.

All cultures have something to contribute to the fabric of the future. Parliament seems a world away and the Church seems to have lost its way against the changing tide of modern values. The violence on the streets of London is really terrible in some places and there just seems that there is no authority capable of dealing with it. I think it would be great to get these kids in a music studio and release their imaginations. The only resource for kids fucked up on drugs and violence is psychiatry and this deeply concerns me.

Psychiatry only serves to re-traumatise the traumatised and imprisons people in a lifetime of institutionalisation, whether prison or the psychiatric ward. Yet here we have in the history of black music art that has risen from the worst of circumstances. The image of Bob Marley rising up through the ground with his dreads comes to mind. Whether Reggae, Funk, or Dance; this art form has driven up from the earth and broken through the barriers. Even if you choose not to use the words spiritual or religious, this music offers a vision of a world full of possibilities and creativity.

The establishment is a distant enigma to the wanderer, but it is failing. I believe the answer lies in the Church; not the tired old fashioned model, but a Church that is open to explore new ideas not least the mysteries of the mind. There is a tale of another outsider that has been ignored by the mainstream and that is Tibet.

Tibet offers a profoundly rich culture and spirituality that is there waiting to be heard. The Church needs to offer refuge for Tibet and listen to what this ancient culture has to say. The world has opened up and a future world needs to reap what every culture has to offer. It is into the mind that Tibet leads us; I put some music on and allow my mind to search the inner universe.

The synth breaks through the speakers like a sonic wind and breathes through my living room. The crisp beats roll out and my mind journeys to a distant horizon.

I've said it before; the English are not a race, we are a people. The English are a people defined by shared values. At this point in the 21st century, we are experiencing a kind of transition from the old to the new. This does not mean that old fashioned values are disregarded but that they are re-interpreted and integrated with new ideas and thoughts.

The height of Anglo-Saxon civilization reached its peak in the early 20th century before great wars fractured the illusion of peace. Following the world wars the British Empire began to dismantle but far from disappearing, the global sphere of Anglo values has formed the Commonwealth; and the UK is now a land rich with cultures from all over the world.

This is a good thing; with these ingredients we can create the future. I have a particular love of people of African and Indian descent. I cannot tell you how important the music has been to me in my life: this music borne from the streets and the harsh realities of black lives. Under extreme pressure coal becomes diamond. The spirituality that India brings to the UK is marvellous and can only help us to re-imagine and improve our own religious culture. John Coltrane was deeply inspired by Indian spirituality – he was a pioneer in the soaring spiritual and searching sound that united the world's cultures.

Alex has an interest in the ancient past of Africa and he has many books about African religions and spiritual traditions. With the rise of modernity the West generally has a sceptical view of religion. It seems that an overtly materialist understanding of the world is dominant. The psychoanalyst Carl Jung saw great value in mythology and spiritual beliefs. For Jung they were an important part of what he called the psyche: the deepest parts of our minds. The cult of rationality and reason only exist on the surface of things; it offers no deep insight into reality.

Psychiatric wards are full of traumatised minds that are wild with hallucinations and psychic thoughts; for the psychiatrist these mind states are just expressions of an illness and that is all. But for someone of Jung's calibre he understood that the expressions of the psyche had meaning that were deeply rooted in an ancient past. Ancient man perceived the world in a mythological language full of symbolic meaning – there was no differentiation between the world outside and that of the mind inside. Alex's perception of danger is real: there is danger out there. His dreams and hallucinations are spiritual in nature and rich in symbolic meaning.

Opening the pages of the history books there are countless images and names of gods that the ancient African believed in. The ancient African lived in a world that was filled with spirits and mystic journeys to other worlds. This, what you might call pagan culture, also existed in ancient Britain with the Celts and the early beliefs of the Anglo-Saxons and Vikings. Carl Jung believed that these ancient cultures still exist deep in our psyches and indeed our modern perception of the world is built on these early foundations.

It is through learning and understanding his ancient past that brings healing to Alex's mind. The music created by the African diaspora in the West is that of a people cut off from their past and history but that is also proof that the reality of the past still exists in the psyche. Jazz, Blues, Funk, and Detroit Techno all exhibit an original sound that came deep from the creative source in the African mind.

The dark winter nights draw in; a strong gust of wind rattles against the windows and breathes heavily through the trees. There is a sense of movement in the air; that primordial energies are shifting and changing. Alex sits smoking a cigarette and we are motionless quiet against the restless sound of the wind. Within the flat there is a stillness; a stillness of thought as we are each absorbed in our own minds.

Here with Alex I feel that our bond of friendship has a great importance for the world. The solution to race relations is not to pretend that there is no difference nor is it to think that our divisions are too great to bridge. The answer is to build a friendship with serious respect for one another and to form an alliance that we can create a better world. We all bring different and equally valuable strengths to the table. There is more to it than this though; on a higher level we are of the same tribe: the future tribe.

On one level we have different backgrounds and history but on another level we share a destiny. Science would have us believe that there is no great meaning to life and that we are mere cogs and wires that have somehow evolved from space dust. The spirituality of Tibet tells us another story; that our lives have arisen from previous lives and that we have journeyed a great distance to meet at this point. This is the calling. That reality is a vast ocean of infinite worlds and each one of us by following our path in the stars has arrived on the shores of this land. Searching for the lost riddim – we follow the rhythm of subtle reality and vibe to the sound of funky beats.

"Man you don't half talk some spaced out funk!" Alex throws a cigarette at me.

"Eh? What d'you mean? This is serious shit I'm talking."

"Yeah man. You're gonna get all voodoo on me. Ha ha!" Alex laughs and rubs his head.
"Well you know voodoo is interesting. That kind of stuff goes deep into time before history."

"Yeah man. I know what you're saying." Alex laughs deeply to himself. "You know, that kind of talk is what the psychiatrists lock people up for."

"Yeah I know. But I'm just interested in the deeper parts of the mind you know. The mind is very complex and I think psychiatry takes a very simplistic view of things."

"Yeah man. But this is the world we're in isn't it? They say slavery has been abolished but all you've gotta do is look at the psychiatric wards and the prisons and you'll see that the African soul is still enslaved." Alex sighs wearily.

"Yeah I think that's true." I reply.

Several weeks have passed since the last visit by the psychiatric nurse; Alex is in a fairly settled place and has enjoyed the respite from the state breathing down his neck. The troubling thing about psychiatry is the threat that it poses to labelling you a danger to society and locking you up with forced treatment. Once this happens it is almost impossible to escape the paralysing force of state institutionalisation.

London is full of troubled minds making their way through the world. For many kids the only choice presented to them is one of drugs and violence; and when they fall the state is there to lock them up either in hospital or prison. There are many good souls on the streets who try to help the kids but it is an impossible task to stop the wave of relentless violence. It seems to me that many young men are taught meaningless drivel in schools and are ill-prepared for the world.

What is the meaning of life? This is a question unanswered in education. The atheism of liberalism tells you there is no meaning whilst the competing religions offer outdated answers. The pallid Church of England is bullied out of significance by the liberals and young men are left alone to orientate their way through a dangerous world. There is no authority that dare pull up the thorns of the rotten ghettoes; it is only the psychiatrist and the police that lie in wait for the disturbed minds.

The religious heritage of the Caribbean is Christian and Alex tells me that his mother is very religious as are many people in Jamaica. For the second generation of West Indians in the UK, their parents' religious beliefs seem outdated. For Alex it was the music that offered him a purpose to life: the music offered a journey through life that was to open many doors. The very best dance music has a spiritual edge that searches higher plains.

The brilliant complexity of Detroit Techno offers an intelligent insight into the mind and searches for a higher meaning. Throughout all of the best black music there is a searching force that seeks a future destination. The rhythm and the funk levitate the mind to a higher consciousness and a deeper vision is discovered.

The 90s seem a long time ago now and although the music is as good as ever the electric vibe of 90s dance culture is yet to be matched. Obviously drugs played a big role in the 90s and I think for a lot of people the negative effects are catching up; but the music has remained unblemished and beneath the haze of ecstasy a pristine music has developed. Sometimes drugs are needed to break out of the restrictive mind-set of the conventional world; but I don't think they're needed anymore. Cigarettes and alcohol are all I need now.

The barren years since the end of the 90s saw the rise and fall of many shit genres and for a while it seemed that the good days were long gone. However, at this point in the 21st century the music is remarkably strong and pioneers such as Alex, now in their 40s and 50s, can offer something very special to the next generation. In all seriousness I think the very best dance music from London and Detroit will last a thousand years. This is the new world; the future.

Alongside his Technics turntables Alex has a whole plethora of futuristic technology such as drum machines and sequencers. The technology is like something from another world. The artist is able to construct and create wild majestic sounds that are something like an ancient magician casting spells. It seems that the prayers of previous generations have culminated in this vision of the 21st century where the artist can explore deep beats rooted in the ancient past and that blast into this world breaking down barriers and forming a new horizon.

It is pioneers such as Alex that can offer a refuge and guidance to the street kids. The stale knowledge of liberalism and the state are defeated by the creative source that searches deep into the soul and sparkles into the new. It would be great to see the street kids lifted out of the gutter and offered the chance to create and release their imaginations.

Alex sits proudly in his chair. He has travelled a great distance and arises in this world as something of a warrior from the heavens. It seems that in this world there is so much that he has to overcome. The very fabric and structure of this society is such that it vilifies his thoughts and behaviour. The prying eyes of psychiatry demonise the rise of anger and imaginative visions; the state seeks to force Alex into conformity and compliance.

Compliance is made at the price of the soul. The forced treatment in the hospitals and detention at her Majesty's pleasure are something of an alien force driving Alex to give in. He sits motionless hidden in the shadows. He smokes a cigarette and his gold jewellery shines against the low light of the lamp. It is as if he exists between two worlds with the distant past behind him and the confrontation of this world before him.

There is still something very old fashioned about British culture. The liberals criticise the anachronism of the Monarchy and the outdated beliefs of the Church. Parliament is dominated by a curious breed of elites that seem alien to the rest of us. If the liberals had their way they would pull down all constructs of the past. This is profoundly ignorant. The traditional structure of the UK is still very relevant but undoubtedly it needs to address the world that surrounds it.

The first method is to re-imagine and revolutionise the Church. The Church needs to explore the mind. The creative studio of the music artist offers a means by which new ideas can be discovered. That the imagination is limitless and that truth is revealed in rhythm and harmony. In his music Alex has discovered the expression of dance and an imaginative vision of what can be brought into the world. Funk unravels the mysteries of reality and offers a way to empower and be in tune with the universe.

The ancient warrior stands by the side of the river and observes the night sky. He sees both the past and the future. The river moves silently and there are darting reflections of life in the forest. The forest vibrates with a subtle rhythm that the warrior understands and follows on his search. Deep in the forest there is movement and dance among the tribe.

In a state of trance, a woman evokes the spirits and gods. There are warnings of danger ahead and guidance for remedies and medicine. A refined vibration moves through the forest; the stars shift and change in pattern and a dragon-like creature appears. The rhythm builds and falls; the beats break and cascade. The eternal dance moves through the night and a timeless vision imagines a path through the danger.

"So your understanding of God is that of some kind of creative source?" I ask Alex. "Is that right?"

"Yeah that's right. You know for many black men the English God has been an alien force making judgement on us. I think this has to change."

"Yeah I agree. The creative source offers a vision that includes everyone. I think though that the fundamental teaching of Christianity on love and compassion are still relevant. It is my view that we need to open up the concept of God and what it means. In Tibetan Buddhism they would call Christ a Bodhisattva – an enlightened being that taught about the nature of reality. Christ taught that love and compassion are fundamental truths about reality. But it seems to me that there is so much more exploration to be done. Christianity in its current form offers a platform to build on – but that's it – there's a whole universe of mystery out there man."

"Yeah. I'm not against Christianity, but you know I feel the

Church offers nothing to me – nonsense from the old-testament that just means nothing. You know, ok, Christ taught us to love one another – but I need more than that – that's not enough to change the world. Christianity needs to be funked up! We need to go deep into the mystery like spiritual adventurers."

In some ways God is the final frontier. Christ taught about the Father – but what is the nature of the Father? It's no good saying we just have to believe and have faith. I want knowledge. Quantum physics is beginning to explore the deeper mysteries of the universe – the paradoxes and counter-intuitive realities. There is no reason why we can't explore the mystery of God. Tibetan Buddhism offers a concept that it calls 'suchness' or 'emptiness'; this concept refers to the very nature of reality that all reality both physical and spiritual are contained within the same source.

The nature of reality is that anything is possible. This means that all phenomena are subject to change and it is through creating the right causes and conditions that we can create change. It is possible to create a reality whereby there is eternal happiness. If this is what we want we can create it. This kind of reality is not some blissed out place where nothing happens – on the contrary a reality free from suffering is one whereby all virtues such as courage and kindness have been perfected.

There is no suffering because suffering has been transformed by bravery into victory. The courage of the spiritual warrior is such that he overcomes fear and attains peace. Motivated by love it is in the midst of battle that the warrior is protected by the shield of courage and the armour of bravery.

The Church offers a foundation to practice and develop the virtues; but it is to us, the future tribe, that we discover the ultimate truth and reality. The means to this discovery is in the music, in art, and all creativity: that we may find new ways of approaching the questions of life and innovate radical new perceptions of reality. The disturbed minds of people in the psychiatric ward are deemed meaningless by psychiatry; but in actual fact such expressions of mind can offer an insight and a sign to a different understanding of life.

I think of the experiences of African Americans in the 60s and 70s when ghettoes were full of drugs and they filled the prisons and psychiatric wards. This is because their minds were not understood by a restrictive western understanding of the mind. That reason and rationality are all and anything that contradicts this or appears to contradict this is criminalised or labelled insane. The slave ships of the 18th and 19th century are symbols of Western ignorance under the command of the god of reason. My point is: the narrow lens of reason cannot capture the vastness and mystery of God or reality.

Alex puts on some sounds: the speakers pulsate with far out breaks and deep rolling bass. This is warrior funk. The beats drive and the synth evokes a dark vibe that all warriors understand; that to defeat evil you have to know evil. The weak and shallow pseudo-compassion of the government and liberals fails because it has no understanding of the true reality of the ghetto.

The warrior funk breaks down barriers and uses fearsome love to reach the street kids. The root of violence on the streets is anger; anger that arises from frustration and no means to expression. The state (whether the police or psychiatry) immediately demonises any show of anger – but the solution lies in channelling this energy. The music offers a way to express our frustration and transform our anger into a creative force.

London is alert to danger. The police scowl the streets with headlights dimmed and hunt for prey. The street kids move through the city with just the whites of their eyes showing in the night air. Knives are hidden loosely in their jacket pockets and they stalk through the streets with expert guile. Danger breathes through the dark; the haters live at night with numbers dialled and deals exchanged. There's some real bad shit out there; people who think nothing of murder.

Alex rose through this world; he knows the gangsters and the haters. There's some bad blood flowing and bad intent eyes Alex's throat. The haters play tricks with the mind and their most powerful weapon is fear. When you step out at night and walk the wet pavements you can feel the bad intent on the cusp of the breeze. You have to watch out for the weasel eyes that peer out from every corner and alleyway ready to deceive and betray. The weak-willed do the haters bidding and the scared (the shook ones) cower to the diktat of the kingpin.

While the ordinary world sleeps; the night wakes with the hum of the dark side of life. Haters like the night because it is when their power is strong; when your power is derived from shadows it is in the shadows when it is most powerful. The weapon of fear is most effective when light is snuffed out and the claws of danger seem to sap your heart of its strength. For the street kids coursing through the city the police offer no refuge; they too are suffused with bad intent.

At night the mind becomes alert and sensitive to the most subtle perceptions. The haters play tricks with the mind evoking paranoia and a loss of understanding what's real and false. The haters smile and befriend you but then you are left with an uneasy feeling as your gut tells you something is wrong. There is a dark force in London that demands its due from Alex; that it's coming for its payment. The rain hits the concrete world outside and a heavy silence surrounds us. You could say paranoia enters our minds as we sit there waiting; but this paranoia is in reality alertness and a heightened perception of darkened energies in the night.

A thick night descends on the forest with a bright full moon in the sky. There are strange sounds that reverberate through the air and coarse cries of night creatures. War is afoot. The warriors paint their faces a thick red and hold their weapons tightly. They walk leaning close to the ground. Nothing is spoken yet they communicate with a collective understanding. The black air is impenetrable to the eye. A rhythm builds and the drums move in time to the steps of the warriors. Their energy grows, the drum patterns shift and the visible world falls away. The spiritual world presents itself and with heightened awareness the warriors step rhythmically and cut through the void.

Alex places the needle of the Technics in the groove of the vinyl; the sonic force breaks through the speakers and fills the room. The smoke of our cigarettes lingers thickly in the air. The force of the night seems to press in on the window and a cold air infiltrates beneath the front door. The music cuts through the black atmosphere and we feel empowered with creative thought. We laugh and talk as the night passes and we go deep into ourselves thinking and dreaming. The music comes out of the speakers like Morse code reaching out to other souls around the world.

A collective consciousness builds and a movement begins to shape the horizon. The sparkle and colour of the music revitalise the night air; the vibe cuts through the dark and opens up a portal to a universe invisible to the hater's eye.

The kettle comes to the boil and I pour the water over the tea bags. The dim light of a cold winter's day impresses through the window. There is a smell of stale smoke that lingers in the room and we sit watching the light chatter of daytime TV.

"There's a lot of shit going on in the world man." Alex says to me.

"Yeah for sure." I reply. "It seems the tectonic plates of the world are re-aligning. War rages in the Middle East and the West is troubled by cultural changes."

"Yeah man."

We sit in silence and smoke, filling the air with a tobacco cloud of contemplation. The bright lights of street Christmas decorations reflect into the room with a strobe effect splintered by the rain. The mechanised hum of the roads resonate a world creaking with the sound of the working day. I get up and look through some of Alex's books. I pull out a photographic book that has pictures of some of the many ancient tribes of Africa.

The images fill me with wonder and give a sense of magical mystery. It is strange to think of these exquisite cultures being subsumed in the hull of a slavery ship. The dull light of the day struggles to light the room and I look over at Alex sitting back in his chair. He smiles and gets up to look through his records. He pulls out the wonderful sleeve of Stevie wonder's Innervisons album which has an image of Stevie cutting through the concrete world with a transcendent vision. The music imagines and creates a different reality.

"You know it's through the music that this ancient culture breaks into the present." I say to Alex.

"Yeah, I think your right. It's like a different reality is breaking into this world. The ancient culture didn't die; it was merely hidden from view. Ha ha. Space funk man."

Through creativity and artistic endeavour the African soul has cut through the suffocating void with the sword of colour and vibrancy. It's like the ancient warrior has travelled through time and come into this dimension.

The grey days continue in a seamless continuum as the build up to the winter festivities intensifies. We are both restless and make our way along the dank pavements into town. The shops are abuzz with fashion conscious shoppers and crowds of tourists. We pay a visit to the Dog and Duck hoping to warm up against the chill winter air. We stand at the bar and Alex laughs as I closely look at the choice of ales on offer.

"Yo man I want to smoke some green not drink this shit!"

"Let's just have a pint mate. It'll warm you up."

I point to my choice and the barman pulls the draught. Alex refuses to have the same and chooses one of the lagers. The pub is small with old wooden interior and memorabilia of London history on the walls. There are a couple of women sitting in the corner and I gesture to Alex that we grab a table not far from where they are. Alex walks tall with his baseball cap tight over his eyes. I unzip my jacket and throw it on one of the seats at the table. We sit down and Alex sits very still drawing the pint glass up to his mouth.

"Cheers my old mate." We tap our glasses together.

"Cheers bruv."

Chapter 5

The ocean travels as far as the eye can see. The horizon seems to curve as the stars sparkle against the restless surface. To the eye of the scientist there is no magic or beauty to the scene; just mechanical reasoning of supposed natural laws. To the artist's eye the horizon offers a thousand stories and conceals a mystery to be discovered. The ocean is full of omens of history that have been and of a future that is to come. Beyond the horizon lie other worlds both beautiful and terrible.

The warrior is a traveller through time and space in search of enlightenment; from one life to the next worlds appear and paths open to new horizons. Beyond time and space there is a dream that imagines a landscape: the traveller courses through the ocean guided by the patterns in the night sky. The scattering of stars present symbols and a language to be understood. The rhythm of the water lapping against the boat moves in harmony with the warm breeze and the movement of the oars.

In search of a future destiny the seeker contemplates the signs and meditates his purpose. That from within his mind a clear light dawns and he follows the secret path to a calling far away.

Deep in the forest there are portents of danger in the air. The atmosphere is thick with suffocating toxicity. From the horizon a darkness looms; the water turns violent with black clouds filling the sky and hard rain falls. A horror pierces the heart of the warrior as he lies watching the fury of the blood soaked sky.

The chains break his skin and dry blood covers his limbs. Something of the world has been fractured and a nightmare enters the forest where once dreams were weaved. A hard skeletal dread surrounds the ships on the shore. It captures his spirit and drives him into the overbearing heat of the prison below. The water beneath the ship moves disturbingly and inharmoniously; it feels impenetrably deep and a dread is carried with the tide. The light of the stars disappear as a new dimension leads to another world.

The beats roll and break; Alex switches the fader bringing two tracks together before reaching down to pull out another record. He manipulates the sound and distorts the airwaves creating a soundscape that energises and inspires the imagination.
The grey air of a winter's day is broken by a rhythmic spell of creative searching. The synth washes and the beats move to the funk creating a magic and power that swallows up the dreary aggressions of small minds.

The creative source discovered within is summoned to pour out like liquid lava in to the physical, solidifying to form new landscapes. Alex stands over the decks with his gold chain hanging low and his head tipped to the side listening to the headphones. He pushes a record back and forth before releasing it to a beat that raises the groove.

"Yeah man I need to get some new clothes. I'm walking round like a fucking tramp at the moment." Alex says loudly.

The designer shops are full of creative materials and Alex pulls on futuristic designs that present an uncompromising style. The clothes confront the world and incite a visual power that stands proud. The style accompanies the sound and raises the call to transform the world. The women look tight in their wear and their erotic power causes the foes to buckle. The sharp beauty of woman calls for a warrior to be strengthened by her love. Only the bravest can understand the power of woman.

Alex rides the threshold cutting beats and heightening consciousness; his path is a dance that re-imagines the world. He holds tight to the rhythm and stays true to his heart. The dancer moves in golden light and empowers the rider; the strength of the sound allows woman to unveil her hidden secrets. Is the rider tough enough? The mysteries of the universe become visible and the funk rides the contours of outer space.

The doorbell rings and Alex gets up to open the front door; a blast of cold air enters which contrasts with the warm smile standing in the door way. The first thing I notice about Lisa are her kind chestnut eyes that have a subtle sparkle to them. She is wrapped up in a thick winter coat with collars that reach up to her chin. She has something of a divine smile and long black hair that has a wholesome gloss as does her caramel skin. Alex quickly invites her in from the cold and embraces her with a heartfelt hug.

"I thought I'd come and see how you are." Lisa explains to Alex. She has a brief glance around the living room and sits down on the sofa.

"So how are you?" She continues.

"Yeah I'm doing ok Lis, thanks." Alex replies lighting up a cigarette. "Things have been pretty dark of late but they're picking up. I appreciate you coming round. How are things with you?"

"Yeah not bad." Lisa responds with a slightly weary tone and she sits back into the sofa glancing over to me with a friendly smile.

"You been looking after him Nathan?"

"I've popped over a few times you know." I inhale the smoke from a cigarette and smile at Alex. "Nothing we can't handle."

Alex sits in close to Lisa and puts his arm around her. She responds and moves in tight to him. I stub my fag in the ashtray

and get up to put my jacket on.
"Ok, I'm gonna get going and leave you two lovebirds in peace."

"Yeah cool man." Alex raises his arm to wave. "Keep in check man; I'll see you tomorrow."

The blast of the winter air hits my face as I open the front door and I make my way into the night.

A whirl of people covers the streets as the late opening hours attract all the Christmas shoppers. The glowing lights colour the high street and there is an expectant air of hope around the corner. I walk alone among a crowd with my thoughts to myself. I am filled with an urge to change the world but I am frustrated at finding a way.

I am an outsider looking in; the smiles and laughter of the shoppers and people sat in cafes are an enigma that I cannot reach. A beggar sits huddled in a worn out sleeping bag and old blankets. I offer him some change; that I feel closer to him than the people around me. The traffic manoeuvres the roads with mechanistic efficiency and people cross the busy highways guiding carefully through the slow moving vehicles. I am a wanderer searching for a way.

The music is my blanket. I listen to the sweet sounds of the folk artist John Martyn and the electronic sound waves from Detroit. I sit alone and smoke through the night deep in meditation and thought. I wonder where things are at now. The 90s are a long time ago and although I miss the ecstasy dance; I am just glad that I got through it in one piece. I am happy now to sit back with a glass of wine and listen closely to the subtle musicianship of the sound craftsmen.

Dance music is here to stay. The musicianship is of the highest order. Detroit is far away but I feel a kinship with the soulful artists. Here in London the cooler than cool Fabio and Grooverider have guided the Drum and Bass scene with expertise; the quality of the music is incredible and I listen at night to the funk masters.

Laura wakes me with a kiss and I smile pulling her close to me. Her shoulders are a smooth golden colour with a perfumed texture. I hold her tight and feel her breasts against my chest.

"What are you doing today?" I ask.

"I've got a few people to see."

I hold her hips and feel the strength of her bones; her legs lie next to mine and I breathe in deep the scent of her body.

The darkness of the early morning begins to recede as the hours pass. I reach for several books from the bookcase and get to reading whilst delighting in a morning smoke.

The ocean lies with a crystal surface reflecting the sunlight. It travels far into the distance and evokes a longing to discover. The universe is a net of jewels that sparkle in a dancing harmony: from one horizon there is another horizon. The traveller carries his wears and seeks kinship with other travellers on the high peaks.

The subtle breeze of reality carries signs and messages – dreams arising from the creative source form worlds and landscapes where the future takes root. The crisp sonic synth fills the room and the artist paints a picture that reaches the minds of others. The beat builds a tempo and raises the energy – the traveller steps to a pace and follows the breeze. Through the dance new forms are carved and colour intensifies. The mind strengthens and gives rise to expansive imagination weaving a complex picture of a future destination.

High in the mountains the warriors traverse dangerous terrain; they move in synchronicity. Their arrows are fixed tight to their backs and their bows are held close to their hips. They stride with a quick pace hardly making a sound except for the blustery wind against the material of their dress. They move stealthily across the rocky paths and climb without rest ever higher into the plains.

Cigarette smoke fills the room. We both sit in serious thought; the wind outside bristles through the streets. Memories of the past echo through our minds – we entered the mandala of the world at different points. My mind is filled with the mythologies of

Northern Europe and the rapacious Germanic tribes crossing the seas to find a new world.

The Germanic god Wodan is a fierce figure with a blood lust and a thirst for alcohol. He is the god of war terrifying to his enemies and hungry for the spoils of wealth. The Celtic myth of King Arthur protects the land and inspires justice throughout his kingdom. Myths are often dismissed as dead modes of belief; but they still exist deep in our psyches.

The hidden memories of the African psyche reveal themselves in the expression of the music. The dub pressure of roots Reggae (amidst a haze of marijuana) releases the Rasta from the constraints of the Babylon world. His mind breathes in the smoke of the herb and the sound waves raise his consciousness to a spiritual plain. It is here that he contacts the antiquity of his psyche; that he remembers a land forgotten and reconnects with history. Within the waking world of slavery the African mind is broken down and enslaved to a false consciousness. Deep in the sound a new horizon rises and the soul is empowered.

I am sure that in Africa there were many different gods and myths unique to each tribe; that there was a god of the sea protecting the seafarers and a god of war that empowered the warriors in battle. The gods are not literal but are symbols of consciousness that represent a different aspect of reality. In the midst of fire, drum rhythms, and dance; consciousness is raised and a deeper reality is unveiled.

Stillness pervades the room; it is dimly lit by a single lamp in the dusk of a winter's day. We cast our minds across the city; it moves busily with restless currents of changing atmosphere. The seasonal shoppers pour through the streets holding two to three bags in one hand. The Christmas lights shine through the damp air and reflect against the shop windows. The city is abuzz with the movement and shifting of commerce.

An alternative view of this world is that of the beggar who sits wrapped in old clothes watching the bustling legs and feet of passers-by. His pockets are empty of money and his mind scours the wet roads for a dry place to sleep. The beggar sees the darker side of life and it is in the dark hours that the underside of consciousness rises to the surface.

Fractured minds lay vulnerable to violence; the shifting flash of sharp blades cut through the air. The dark minds drive slowly through the streets; lights dimmed and callous eyes reaching out of lowered windows. Broken minds are found in houses both rich and poor. It is usually with drugs that a person is seduced into a darker world and they succumb to fear unable to escape. The bad men are heavily built with lifeless eyes and an ability to overawe people with an illusion of power. They are experts at breaking fragile minds and with a tight grip they draw people into their domain.

Alex knows this world and the night breeze carries a sinister whisper that attempts but fails to draw him in. The colourful beats break against the air and force a lighter atmosphere in to the murkiness. The rhythm and melody fill the breaks with a cosmic vision that inspires the soul to strengthen.

"So what's your interest in Tibet Nathan?"

"I discovered it when I was searching for some kind of refuge."

"That's interesting man. I don't know a lot about it. But you seem to know a thing or two."

"I'm no expert mate, but it's got me thinking you know. The story of Tibet is a hidden tragedy that the world knows little about. The Tibetan people have been crushed by a dark force. Their lives have been suffocated by a monstrous violence. But the philosophy is so rich you know. It's really incredible."

"Yeah man. It sounds interesting. I like the idea of going deep into the mind. That's my bag man – I wanna go deep. Ha ha ha. Would you say that you're a Buddhist?"

"No man. I'm not a Buddhist. I want to bring in some of these ideas into English culture you know. It seems to me that Christianity doesn't give much of an explanation of what God is and Tibetan philosophy provides some good ideas."

"Yeah man, I hear what you're saying. I'm not sure about religion though bro. I'm not against it – I just feel there's not much there for me."

"Yeah man, I understand that. The thing about Tibetan philosophy is that it frees you from believing in anything outside of yourself: it's all about discovering your own potential within. It's about tapping into the creative source you know."

"So where is the creative source? In the mind?"

"Yeah, in the mind."

"And the idea is that anything is possible?"

"Anything is possible."

"I like that man." Alex laughs.

Following the festivities of Christmas and New Year, the first working week of January brings some respite and calm. The year ahead unfolds like a mountainous landscape with many journeys to come. We sit together smoking amidst the buzz of the TV; Alex stares directly at the TV as I listen to the whirring sound of traffic outside. Despite the settled air, it feels that there is a battle to be won against the dark forces. It is perhaps a battle too big for either of us, but we rest in our minds and contemplate the unfolding path that lies ahead.

Alex plays some fresh new music; we laugh and joke together as the short winter day draws in. As the music fades there is a sound of traffic loudly passing by which soon tails off into a low distant murmur. Alex has an upcoming appointment with the psychiatrist; he is in a stronger place at the moment but he is still anxious about the meeting.

The glistening water of the ocean reflects the flickering light of the night sky. There is a stillness but it is tempered by a portent of things to come. The ocean seems to stretch out into the horizon without limit. The horizon curves and the light of the moon rests on high clouds. Beneath the shadow of the clouds, there is a depth to the horizon that is both beautiful and ominous. The journey of the spiritual warrior is one filled with beauty but also great danger.

"So, I've got this appointment next week." Alex tells me.

"Yeah man, how you feeling about it?"

"I'm alright man. It's just something I don't need; you know? It's been some mad few weeks. I've just got to keep my head up."

"Yeah mate."

There is a shuffle of delicate feet outside before the doorbell rings and Alex opens it to the warm smile of Lisa. Her eyes sparkle as she says hello and takes her coat off.

Alex sits on the sofa with his arm hanging loosely around Lisa's shoulders and he talks with a relaxed and calm temper.

"So how are things with you?" I ask Lisa.
"Oh, all good Nathan."

Alex pulls her in tight to him and she laughs gently smiling with bright white teeth. Her jewellery rustles as she sits in close to Alex.

"I was just saying to Nathan that I've got another appointment with the psychiatrist next week."

"Yeah, so how are you feeling?" Lisa replies.

"I'm good you know. I'm just fed up of this shit."

Alex gets up to put some music on. I throw a cigarette over to Lisa and we both light up. Alex pulls out a few old Soul records and we sit back enjoying the sound.

The forest rustles in unison to the breeze; dark heavy clouds gather in the distance as a slow clap of thunder echoes through the sky. The rain begins to pour down and the warriors take cover. On the horizon what appear to be skeleton ships move deliberately towards the shoreline. The ships are hard to see and covered by shadows. The world is taking shape as the portents of history enslave the soul captives. The rain pours down and amidst distorted sight naked bodies are bound in chains. Western man has conquered the seas and he takes his financial gain back to the old world. Deep in the hull the soul captive breathes in the toxic air and searches in his mind for liberation.

The psychiatrist sits with pen in hand making notes. There is no warmth to his manner but occasional nods that offer a pretence of understanding. The room seems to push in on Alex and he finds it hard to breathe. The psychiatrist looks closely at him as if regarding some kind of scientific experiment. Alex's mind is wild with paranoia and anxiety. He sits motionless but inside his mind is in a torrent.

With a piercing stare and holding a pen it is as if the doctor holds a knife to Alex's throat. He looks directly at the doctor without moving and continues to explain how he is feeling. The doctor pulls back and without speaking he furiously writes down some notes before concluding the meeting.

Lisa pulls Alex in close to her and kisses his cheek. Alex rests sitting back in the sofa smoking. The smoke rises from his silent frame and contorts into a swirling cloud as it rises to the ceiling. The flat is dark and the sound of the busy streets fall muffled against the window. Outside the low winter light is pierced by the glaring lights of head lamps and red tails. The pavement is hardened by walking bodies and the veins of traffic filter throughout the city.

Laura pushes her thigh over my waist and I pull her in towards me. I lie back with my arm behind my head staring up at the morning sunlight breaking through the curtains. So much trouble in the world rings through my mind (the words of Bob Marley). The first thing I do in the morning is throw some teabags in a pot and have a good smoke. There is something about that first cigarette of the day. I flick through the morning news programmes and blowing smoke into the air I contemplate the day ahead.

I feel powerless to help Alex. The body of psychiatric knowledge in society is such that it has the full weight of law behind it. I am not completely against psychiatry but I just feel that the treatment is so often very lacking in empathy. In some ways Alex is unwell, but that is not to say that there is no meaning to what he is experiencing. There is that well-known line that just because I am paranoid doesn't mean that they're not after me. Psychiatry could play a very supportive role but by denying the meaning of Alex's experience and the reality of danger that exists in the world; it is only serving to further disempower Alex from the authenticity of his own mind. It is another brick in the wall.

My own life is filled with music and contemplation of deeper things. My mind has scoured wide and far for spiritual yearnings and religious fulfilment. At times this has left me open to the charge of mental illness as my mind goes a little haywire in search of deeper truth. It is with Tibet that I have found the most insightful understanding of reality: that the truth lies deep within our minds. The outward expression of a Christian faith towards a God 'out there' seems to ring hollow not just with me but with so much of modern society.

Tibet teaches us to search inward for meaning and salvation. I do not identify as a Buddhist; rather I want to use the inspiration of Tibet to transform my own culture and society. At this point in time, it seems that we are at a cross-road of change as a people. Here in England I am beginning to perceive a mandala (a symbolic picture of reality) that is taking shape. Here we have people from all over the world gathering to make a life for themselves on this small island.

I think if managed correctly this point in time can herald a great vision of a future world that takes the best from all the cultures and creates something both complex and beautiful. In Alex I see an incredible spirit rich in spiritual understanding and of course the most incredible music. There are other cultures like Indian that offer the most amazing spiritual heritage and the best food in the world. We need to weave these ingredients and form a new horizon.

The evening approaches and Laura brings in a plate of food handing it to me. She sits next to me and we watch the TV.

"This is nice babe. Thanks a lot."

Laura moves her head from side to side and her bronze hair flickers across her neck and shoulders. She seems distant from me. She is sitting slightly in front of me on the sofa and I notice her gentle back with her shoulder blades moving as she eats. I run my hand down her spine and she reacts by telling me with a full mouth of food to leave off. As quick as she sat down she gets up and takes her plate to the kitchen.

"So how is Alex?" Laura asks when she comes back in the room. "Yeah, he's alright. It's a difficult situation you know. I mean, yeah he is unwell in a certain way; but I just feel the system brings him down."

Laura sits in close to me and holds a glass of wine close to her chest. I flick through the TV channels seeing what's on, but Laura quickly grabs the remote from me and with an exasperation of frustration she settles on one channel. I sit back and drink my wine laughing.

Laura pulls in close to me; "what is it you're trying to solve with Alex?"

"What do you mean?"

"Oh, I just feel that you're consumed with helping him but it is not clear to me what exactly is going on."

"Well, he's unwell you might say."

"So why can't the doctor just deal with it?"

"Because they see no value in what he is experiencing. You know, there is darkness out there. The psychiatrist just wants to force Alex into conformity and denies all validity of his thoughts. I think this is wrong."

"Don't you think you're getting a little drawn in; that you too might start being called ill?"
I turn and look at Laura, "why do you think I'm getting ill?"

She avoids my gaze and looking past me she says, "no, I just worry that you're being drawn into something that is quite dangerous."

"No, no, no; there's nothing to worry about."

The horizon rises and amidst the high snowy peaks, we lean close to the ground and track our path. The beauty of the environment is only matched by the danger that surrounds us. We course a journey together navigating our destination with the pattern of stars in the sky. This dream exists beyond time in a place before the current world existed: that we may envision a future and forge an ocean that collects the tales of every river. The universe is ours and with musical rhythm we traverse the heights to the new world.

Alex pulls his head back and staring up at the ceiling he lets out a bellowing laugh. I laugh with him and lighting up a cigarette I throw a lighter at him to shut him up. The bright light of the New Year shines through the flat windows and amidst a haze of smoke we talk like warriors among the heightened folds of the world. We sit quietly together as we watch events unfold around us.

The staring glint of sharp knives pierces the settled consciousness of our minds; that danger is reminding us of its presence in London town. Beneath the hum of a January traffic there lays a restless energy that is lustful to fill its appetite. The ghosts move in unison around the town and the hard lifeless eyes of the haters sharpen through the walls. Alex sits motionless and stares unblinking directly at the dark figures.

We exist in a kind of twilight of consciousness whereby we watch the dark shadows move through the air but we know all too well that this perception will be deemed schizophrenic. So it is a balancing act; we rest on the high peaks and watch the bodies move heavily but we do not move. Outside the cold air presses hard against the wrapped up bodies and ill-intent scours the worn streets. Ill-intent filters through the wind and finds vulnerable souls to haunt and cajole into negative acts.

Clouds high up far in the sky begin to cover the last rays of sunlight. There is an eagle that flies just beneath the clouds and we watch as it makes a circled descent before dropping sharply to the ground. We do not see if it caught its prey or not. The air is very cold but dry; the weathered and worn mountains speak of many tales and the wind washes over them and witnesses our travel.

It is early evening and we sit in the living room watching the TV. Alex rests in the shadow of the room and draws loosely on a cigarette hanging out of his mouth. I too draw on a cigarette and we sit together sensitive to every noise that we hear. The wind clamours at the door and windows; the forces of nature seem to bang on the walls outside and some kind of animal makes a screeching cry before fading into the distance.

The hater stands obscured beneath the high collars of his jacket; he stands with attentive soldiers around him and he pays us a visit. His hands are laden heavy with gold and he holds a large knife tightly. The knife appears filthy and has a surface that is jagged and vile. The hater moves his other hand through his jacket pockets and pulls out several dirty polythene bags that are filled with a mushy brown powder.

"You wanna have some of this in yer Alex eh?"

Alex does not answer and the hater draws up close to him with a smile that reeks of rotten decay. He smiles and laughs; the hyenas that stand with him join in with the filthy laughter. The knife is drawn up close to Alex's throat and the brown bags pushed under his nose.

"I'll get ya, you wait matey."

The cold winter evening draws in; the flat is lit poorly and the muted screen of the TV displays moving images that have a strobe effect of flickering light. Alex rests in a covering of shadows which are only pierced by the glow of his cigarette. I sit with him and listen to the wind blowing against the windows and a distant siren trailing away along an unknown street. Alex gives out a wide grin as if laughing at the madness of it all. He smokes the cigarette and snorts before coughing repeatedly.

"Them gangsters want a piece, don't they?" Alex says to me leaning in slowly.

"It's just your mind man, don't worry too much about it."

"Yeah. It's just my mind. Yeah, that's right."

Alex stands up slowly and moves through to the kitchen to make some coffee. I sit staring at the silent TV screen and light up another fag.

Chapter 6

Laura walks into the bedroom wearing just a pair of thin knickers. I pull her in towards me and feel the soft texture of her thigh. She leans in to me and gently breathes close to my neck; I pull her long hair down across the front of her collar bone. I feel the warmth and beauty of her body; her soul is like a vibrant electricity breathing into me. The world falls away and we unify in a cosmic dance of liberty. I hold her with my strength and the curves of her being enliven my spirit.

The winds of dharma from the Tibetan mountains breathe through my soul but I am lost to find an expression for this in modern language. I am attracted to the work of idealist philosophy; that reality is discovered within the mind and that the physical is an expression of the inner. The dominant materialist thinking of the modern world jars against my thinking and I sit back smoking and dreaming.

That within the mind is an epic of adventure; that there lies the true journey and destination. That dreams are meaningful and even the expressions of a madman has value. I strongly feel that the apparent insane behaviour of the bodies in the psychiatric ward offer a kind of mandala of reality: that is they offer a puzzle which needs to be deciphered and can show us a greater understanding of reality.

Laura sits next to me with a coffee cupped between her hands. She is dressed only in her dressing gown and even in the most ordinary situation I think she is beautiful.

The sunlight pours through the open window; Alex is up, dressed, and smiling.

"Yo, boy! What you up to man?!"

"Yeah, what are you up to mate?" I reply.

The Detroit flavours push through the speakers and an air of good vibes spreads around the environment. Creativity is the way to beat the haters.

Alex is dressed well and full of energy; he grabs me round the neck and says that we're going out.

"Where to man?"

"I'm gonna go up the West End for a bit."

"Alright."

The city in the New Year is abuzz with movement and change; the veins of traffic spread throughout the concrete jungle and walkers jostle for space on the busy high streets. It seems that the whole world is here in London; we cross the busy highways and head to a local café. Alex is in a good mood but his movements are still slow and languid. We sit down and gather our thoughts. With an espresso each and a suitable ashtray we watch the swathes of different faces move through the crowd.

"How you feelin' man?" I ask Alex.

"Yeah, I'm alright man. Just got a fucking running nose. I must have a cold or something."

"Yeah man, I feel a bit rough myself. What's the plan then?"

"I reckon just check out a few clothes shops – that's all."

"Cool."

Alex is a cool cat and he sits back with his baseball cap tight over his eyes. He wears a thick black jacket and some spaced out trainers. He seems to sit removed from the world; as if he is watching from afar. Occasionally he reaches in to me and tells a joke or something and then leans back cool as anything. The pavement is awash with hundreds of people moving like salmon through the stream. From time to time a pretty woman catches one of our eyes. Alex points out something about someone and we both crack up with laughter before deciding to head to some clothes shops.

Alex stands staring in the mirror like some futuristic space man. He pulls on the designer threads and with a high collar he walks back and forth against the mirror.

"Yeah, I like this man. Some spaced out funk."

It seems to me that the music goes hand in hand with fashion. It's all about creativity and expression. We're on the futurist tip; that an imagined destination is coming to fruition. Alex breaks into a dance before laughing loudly and we bang our shoulders together before going out to look at some more space wear.

Awash on the horizon there are portents of things to come: that dreams collide and a future is made. The seekers stand tall against the strong breeze and in the distance there are signs of a land forming. That the land is formed by our minds and the contents of the world are made from dreams. The warrior moves swiftly across the terrain. Before the sunrise there is darkness and the ghost ships move through the blood red sea; but the seed of the future is hidden deep within.

Alex stands looking in the mirror back at his place and he seems happy with his purchase. He puts on some sounds and we bathe our minds in the electronic sonic force. He feeds the sound through some digital machines and creates a unique beat that jars against the cold outside and forms a vibe that is cutting edge. Electronic music has the same vibe as punk that stands against the current streams of society and refuses to conform. Alex is a digital punk and the colour of the sound enlivens the atmosphere.

The cold air pushes through my jacket as I make my way to Alex's. The low light of a winter's day keeps everyone covered beneath scarves and hoods; the orange glow of the street lights glimmer against the drizzle of the spitting rain and I tread carefully crossing the busy roads to my destination.

Alex opens the door with a gentle smile and leads me slowly into the living room. The good vibes of the day before have softened into a somewhat melancholic acceptance of things. That is; the dark days still draw on. Alex keeps the flat dimly lit and we sit together listening to some ambient sounds. The beats and sonic melody guide our minds through a meditation that we might find some answers. The music takes us away from the grime of London life and envisions a dream world of infinite potential.

The clouds clear in the sky and a flock of large birds fly gracefully through the air. The seekers rest high on the peaks and witness the blood ships move silently through the sea; that they creak and break against the sharp waves. Our witness is that of two friends seeing the unfolding of history; that the darkness moves in stealthily and retreats over the horizon with sinister quiet.

The psychiatrist demonises Alex's behaviour; he talks of hallucinations and the danger posed by Alex's temper. The haters pour through the cracks of the walls and haunt the fractured air. They circle round stealing the oxygen and tightening their grip. The rain hits against the window and it is cold. The blood soaked movements of the killers leave an ugly trail in the hallway. The polythene bags of drugs are cut open and tasted; the dark alleyways of London lie full of half living creatures with sullen eyes that pierce the apparent calm of night.

Alex sits in deep and as usual he is hidden behind the shadows of the living room. The haters move around him and threaten him with violence, but he sits tight and blows tobacco smoke towards the ceiling. The wet streets outside reverberate with ceaseless traffic and bodies finding their way through the evening. The psychiatrist sits in his office and contemplates the delusions and mental illness of his clients. That with the right medication they can be brought in to good order and detained in the hospital they might mechanically change their behaviour.

The danger is real; it moves in the night air and with the cold breeze. The haters circle Alex and place a sharp blade against his neck. The haters arise from the dark side of consciousness that is unseen and unrecognised by the wider world. The drugs run around the city streets and float along the streams of the gutter.

The African slave is thrown into this world and without guidance they navigate their way through this dangerous terrain.

I rest my mind in the sound. It seems to me that darkness arises from the mind; that it is the aspect of the mind that is wild and untamed. Although Alex is unwell in some ways, the danger that he is witnessing is very real. The danger of the London streets reverberates through the city and people get caught up in it and sometimes killed. These bodies find their way to the psychiatric ward where they are labelled mentally ill and subjected to a harmful treatment. I think the answer for Alex lies in the unravelling of his imagination and his dreams.

The river moves towards the forest and the silent warriors stand in maroon cloth waiting for the boat to arrive. They move gracefully and without sound. They seem to be at one with their environment and hardly create a ripple on the surface of the water as they pull the boat to shore. The forest rustles with a gentle breeze and Alex is taken by hand and led inwards to the forest. The tribe are colourful and beautiful; there is a soft vibration of harmonious energy and the seeker is placed within a room and allowed to rest. Communication amongst the tribe is like a gentle vibration that moves through the air and the natural environment offers respite from a war-torn world.

Alex smiles and throws me a cigarette. The flat remains dimly lit but our mood lifts and the flashing screen of the TV evokes a colourful strobe against our dark bodies. The music breaks the air in the room and our minds awaken to an imaginative vision. The mundane falls away and we raise our conversation talking about things to come and dreams to be fulfilled.

"Where do you think we're heading man?" Alex asks.
"What do you mean?"

"I mean, where's the world at? What's the future?"

"Who knows man?"

Alex laughs and replies, "I think the future is about raising consciousness you know. About believing in things that we can achieve."

"Yeah, I hear that."

"It's about the creative source man."

"Yeah man I like that."

"Do you think the creative source has something to do with ancient African culture Nathan?"

"Yeah, you know what, I do. I think ancient African tribes were totally in tune with the creative source. I think that is what all the music and the funk are about."

"Yeah, I kind of understand that."

The electronic vibes push through the air and break the physical into the spiritual. The coloured sounds of the synth sparkle and invoke our imagination. Alex gets up and looks through some records. He pulls out a few old white labels and listens to how they sound. The crackling intros remind us of earlier years and bring a smile to my face as I remember the good feelings.

The night is full of danger and the DJ knows this all too well. The club is full and the women are dancing. Faces and bodies move through the strobe light and every look tells a story. The gangsters stand at the back and occasionally move through the crowd selling their wares. It was all part of the scene; the danger was part of the scene. In a way that is what made it exciting but only to a point. You see the haters don't get the vibe. They push on through the crowds but it is blood that they want. They want power over people and like people being afraid of them.

Back in the day there were all sorts of characters on the scene. The drugs played their role but they spoke of an underworld that occasionally sought its due. Alex was a popular guy on the scene but there was no escaping the darker side of things. These characters made their way through people and at times Alex had to deal with these shadow figures. The drugs have a way of not letting you go and reminding you that they were a part of your life. Growing up on the rough streets of South London for someone like Alex they had no choice but to brush shoulders with the haters.

The drug days are gone, but something haunts Alex's mind. My understanding is that his tale is that of a survivor who has come up through the streets but who the streets haven't quite left behind. The music is the gift of the African diaspora, but it has arisen from tough lives. The psychiatrist is just another enemy to deal with as Alex finds his way to the surface. The psychiatrist denies Alex his story and only serves to demonise the healing response of his psyche; that the mind responds by dreams and imagination to heal itself.

It's early morning and Alex is resting on the sofa with Lisa; he holds her in an embrace and they seem to be half asleep close to one another. The air is cold outside and the poorly heated flat allows a draft to run through. Alex wakes Lisa and they move to the bedroom. Taking their clothes off, they hold each other tightly soaking in the warmth of the other body. Alex is a little over weight from the medication, but he still has a strong muscular frame. Lisa is a petite girl with a thin body and she rubs her hands over Alex. The early morning is still dark and the cold breezes in as they huddle together beneath the covers.
I lie with Laura awake in the early hours thinking about the day ahead. Laura leans over to me and kisses me. I hold the back of her neck placing my hand beneath her hair and breathe close to her. She moves in to me and arches back revealing the sculpture of her breasts and stomach. I sit up to hold her; she responds by coming in to me and then she pulls back. There is something that I cannot understand. She pulls away from me and leaves the room. I lie back with my arm behind my head staring at the open door.

Laura seems to move in and out of my sight.

I begin to think how life is something of an adventure; that we are merely travellers passing through. The people we meet and the situations we face are all lessons to be learnt that we may grow as people and strive on to further worlds. My thinking is clearly influenced by Tibetan Buddhism, but I rest my mind thinking that these views are something of a novelty in the modern world. My relationship with Alex is based on something deeper than just having met in this life; that through our previous lives we created the conditions to meet in this world. We are dreamers and we dream of a future world that is wakeful to creativity and the imagination. I want to be an artist and create. I want to enjoy the fruits of the world and delight in the company of others.

Laura wakes and dresses for work. Damn, she looks sexy in her tight little skirt. She berates me for staring with my tongue hanging out. My wolf-like masculinity wants to rip her clothes off but she walks past my lust and throws yesterday's post at me. It seems to me that the power of woman lies in her eroticism but Laura gets angry with me when I say this. She stands tall, prim, and proper; frustrated with me she leans in to kiss me and breaks my balls with her cold stare. The dance with woman continues apace and I sit back lighting a cigarette.

Lisa wakes with Alex and she rubs her hand across his face. He lies deep in himself and his strong chest rises with each breath. Lisa is anxious for him, but Alex is calm inside and like a great

hero he holds Lisa tight and fills her with warmth. The danger lingers uneasily on the cold air and it feels that the locks on the door are almost useless. The gangsters want their due and darkness penetrates the atmosphere.
"Don't worry babe." Alex whispers to Lisa.
"Them haters can't break me."

Lisa offers no reply and rests her head on Alex's shoulder breathing gently against his skin.

The drugs don't sleep but find their way from one hand to the next. They invite willing partners to an illusion of power and wealth. The top dogs enjoy the luxuries of houses and cars; the street pushers are merely trapped within the system and like wild animals they just seek self-preservation from one day to the next. The pusherman is filled with jealousy and rage that no nigga is going to be bigger than him. He sends out his troops and listens for word on the streets. There's a guy that owes him some due and with mind filled with malice he seeks to haunt them and take what's his.

Alex rose up from the streets and as such there is a part of them that are still with him. He is breaking free but his mind is haunted by the darker side of that life. The danger and the violence. The powder and the blades. The streets don't want to let him go; he lies motionless on his bed and the darkness creeps up like an enemy dressed up as an old friend. He takes his medication, but although they lessen some of the anxiety they do not cure the mind. The cure lies in understanding his mind and unravelling the story that he has travelled.

The drum rhythms build and fall spreading throughout the forest. They carry tales and myths of a people who have travelled through long distances and time. Women nourish and nurture the tribe; they also offer dance and mystical prayers to the gods that waken the forest to another vision. The women are the symbol of fearlessness that the warriors carry with them into battle. Woman is the source of the warrior's strength. Lisa gets up from the bed; her small pert breasts reveal delicately against the morning sunlight.

The day is bright with sunlight but the air is cold; I make my way to see Alex hoping that he is feeling better. He opens the door with a mischievous smile and I shake his hand laughing at his grin.

"What are you so happy about?" I ask.

"What d'you mean mate? Can't a man smile?"

"Yeah, but that was no fuckin smile! Ha ha ha!"

"Yeah, alright mate. What d'you want? Tea or coffee?"

"Tea mate. English Breakfast."

I have a look at the vinyl spinning on the turntable and then sit down in front of the TV. The afternoon news displays all manner of confusion going on in the world.

"World's fucked up mate." Alex says handing me the tea.

"Yeah man, there's a lot of problems."

The sunlight breaks through the drawn curtains and the flat seems to gratefully soak in the sunshine. It is cold though and I sit keeping my jacket on. Alex sits down on the sofa and leans back into the corner. He does not say anything but sips his tea and sniffs from time to time.

The ambient sound of Drum n Bass on the turntable begins to fade out and Alex gets up to put another record on.
Sitting down again Alex leans forward and asks me, "You know we were talking about the creative source and all that?"

"Yeah." I reply.

"I like that kind of thinking man."

"Yeah, so do I."

"I definitely think some of these ideas are rooted in Africa."

"Yeah, I think so as well. It's about energy I think: creating good energy."

"Yeah man. I agree with that." Alex leans back into the sofa and sniffs a couple of times before lighting a cigarette.

The seeker approaches the forest. There is silence and a deep sense of life among the trees. A man and woman dance to a rhythm that pulsates higher and higher before calming to a hypnotic slow beat. In these moments what you might call prayers are uttered. The unconscious is expressed and symbols are formed. From this the reality of life unfolds.

Printed in Great Britain
by Amazon